Praise

MW00423055

"Who has not drea
the distant past reappears... In *The Last First Kiss*, she shows up to visit the septuagenarian widower at his old family beach house on the Outer Banks of North Carolina. Here is the story of an American generation, the '60s, of all our lost young loves, and a brilliant meditation on the passing and relevance of time. An approaching hurricane adds increasing drama to the revelations from the past and the growing attraction between these two absolutely real and deeply drawn characters. Walter Bennett has written a compulsively readable novel that rings true all the way through."

–Lee Smith, author of *On Agate Hill*
and *Dimestore: A Writer's Life*

"The question is not if *The Last First Kiss* is the most necessary, heartbreakingly honest, profoundly moving novel in years, but why this is so. The book has everything a good novel needs: compelling characters so real you have the sensation they are old friends, a story that is at once romantic, precise, and without one whiff of the delusional. It is a story that leads to the deepest, most human sense of recognition. *The Last First Kiss* is for anyone who has fallen in love when young and thought about it later and longed for a second chance. I've read very few books that were equal to a line from T.S. Eliot—"mixing memory and desire"—but *The Last First Kiss* is surely one of them. If you are grownup, you need this book now, and if you are young, you will need it soon."

– Craig Nova, author of *The Good Son* and *Cruisers*

"*The Last First Kiss* is the generous-hearted story of a man and a woman in their seventies, who spend a weekend together in an old beach house, hoping to escape the confusion and pain in their pasts, looking to create something clarifying, even intimate, for the future. There are egrets and herons in these pages, 'a large doe crossing a finger of water.' They form the backdrop for this engaging tale about the power and pull of memory, the power and pull of love. I was totally enthralled."

— **Judy Goldman**, author of *A Memoir of a Marriage and a Medical Mishap*

"Walter Bennett's literary range is startling. From the surefooted *Leaving Tuscaloosa*, a coming-of-age novel set in Civil Rights era Alabama, to this new novel, *The Last First Kiss*. At first blush it seems like a beach romance between old sweethearts with the menace of an impending hurricane adding tension to their reunion. But Bennett rips the covers off their comfort as they revisit the fifty-some years they did not share. He writes with utter authority."

— **Georgann Eubanks**, author of *Literary Trails of North Carolina* and *Saving the Wild South: The Fight for Native Plants on the Brink of Extinction*

"Walter Bennett's *The Last First Kiss* is a true gem of a novel, finely cut, brilliantly polished, and chosen from excellent stone. He's taken what could have been a simple love story and imbued it with such honesty, originality, and sincerity that it rises above its genre and into rarely visited territory. Bennett ventures bravely into aspects of life—aging, regret, imperfection, doubt— that most writers glide across or avoid entirely. I admired this book greatly and enjoyed it from first page to last."

— **Roland Merullo**, author of *Breakfast with Buddha* and *A Little Love Story*

The Last First Kiss

Walter Bennett

LYSTRA BOOKS
&c Literary Services

The Last First Kiss
Copyright © 2021 by Walter Bennett
All rights reserved

ISBN paperback, 978-1-7336816-9-8
ISBN ebook, 978-1-7363055-0-8
Library of Congress Control Number: 2020924407

The Last First Kiss is a work of fiction. Names, characters, places, and incidents are either the product of the author's imagination or are used fictitiously. Any resemblance to actual persons, living or dead, events, or locales is coincidental.

Except for brief excerpts used in reviews, neither this book nor any of the contents may be reproduced in any medium or form without written permission. Please direct requests to the publisher as shown below.

Author's photo by Betsy Bennett

Book design by Kelly Prelipp Lojk

Published by Lystra Books & Literary Services, LLC
391 Lystra Estates Drive, Chapel Hill, NC 27517
lystrabooks@gmail.com

To fellow travelers on the rim of light:
eyes straight ahead, nose to the wind;
keep moving as fast as you can.

When we talk about the past,
we lie with every breath we draw.

—William Maxwell

Thursday evening, near dusk

Ace Sinclair dons a fleece jacket and Red Sox cap and takes his highball glass and fifth of single malt to the roof deck of his beach house overlooking the sea. Before she died, his wife, Pam, and he followed this same ritual. It provided them serenity, a day's-end, quiet intimacy. Now it's just him, the sea, the sky, and the darkening woods. But something from those old times with her hovers like the evening's last gull over the sunset glow in the slow-breaking waves. It would feel like a betrayal to miss it.

His house faces northeast. A hundred years ago, his grandfather sited it in a cove on Pomeiooc Island off the North Carolina coast, where the seaward shoreline curves briefly eastward, slips around a point, and dips south again. A hiding place, his grandfather used to say, from Atlantic storms, tucked safely into its grove of yaupon and live oak. But for Ace, the main advantage is the line of sight from the deck.

When the sun sets and the ocean darkens, he can turn to face north and watch headlights of cars pop above the crest of the Crowbank Inlet Bridge two miles away. The lights flow toward him down the slope of the bridge and across the long causeway, only to wink out among the shadowy dunes that line the island shore—a ceaseless caravan headed to the hotels and condos crowding beaches to the south. If he drinks enough single malt—at his age it only takes a couple of glasses—the caravan begins to flow as if from the ancient tales his grandmother read to him as a kid, downstairs in this very house. Time swirls and blends. The woods around him, full of night sounds, and the ocean, washing the beach beyond the dunes, become the real world. The rest of his life, trapped in the shaded memories and the old furniture in his house in Raleigh, vanishes.

On nights when the moon is full and the tide is high, he swears he can feel the island move.

He pauses at the railing to pour himself a couple fingers of Scotch, then moves his chair so he can watch the slow-moving headlights. They seem brighter than usual, more urgent, the night settling around them darker than in evenings past. Out there beyond the breakers, a storm is building—or *re*building—as it bides its time, trying to decide where to hit next after trashing Cuba and much of the Caribbean. Ace heard about it on the morning news; Freya, they call it, after the Norse goddess of love. (What idiot, for God's sake, thought of that one?) It could go anywhere, the weather guy said. *Straight this way*, a voice in the back of Ace's head whispers.

"So typical of you," Pam would have said. "How did you get to be such a pessimist?"

"I'm a Red Sox fan," he would answer.

"Calvinism," she would say. "The alligator in your Scottish gene pool."

But Freya will probably come to nothing. It's well into October, and a lot of these late storms peter out or turn and head out to sea.

He settles into the chair, takes a deep breath, and raises his glass for a sip. The now familiar tremor hits his hand and rattles the glass rim against his bottom teeth. He lowers the glass to avoid a slosh onto his chest. Hell, he's seventy-five—of course he has a few shakes now and then. He shifts the drink to his other hand and tries again. The aromatic warmth swells in his throat as the liquor goes down, that welcome soothing of tissue and easing of mind. Another deep breath, a sigh.

Eighteen, twenty hours, and she will be here—J'nelle Reade—flying from New York to Raleigh, where she will rent a car and drive eastward through the vast coastal plain of North Carolina to Pomeiooc Island, then turn south, and eventually cross the very inlet bridge that feeds that stream of headlights moving toward him now. Except by then, of course, it will be tomorrow afternoon, and if he loosens his mind a bit, lubricates it with enough Scotch, that can still seem very far away, almost receding.

Except that she is not receding, she is coming. And how, exactly, did he get himself into this visit, this, well, situation?

He and J'nelle have lived a couple of hour's plane flight from each other most of their lives. Until a few months ago, they had not communicated in decades except for

3

small talk at a few high school reunions in Layton, Alabama, and an email correspondence that flared for a while, then seemed to burn itself out. He'd begun it to express condolences when he heard her husband, Seth, had died. Actually, Seth was only *presumed* to have died, vanished on a solo motorcycle trip to Alaska. The search went on for months, checking motels and cafes, scouring mountain ravines. It seemed strange to Ace that a guy Seth's age would take off alone on a long-distance motorcycle trip. And that vanishing, that gone-to-nowhere, Ace imagined, might leave an even deeper hole than that left by certain knowledge of death. Pam had been dead several years by then, and suddenly, the clarity and certainty of that were a comfort.

So he'd been surprised a month ago when, out of the blue, she emailed what she called a "quick check-in" that wasn't quick at all but more an internal review of her life that he'd heard only fragments of before in their previous emails about Seth: her college career (floundering at first but stellar by the end), a tour in the Peace Corps, grad school, then more Peace Corps (apparently something of a big shot, running programs in various countries), similar work for the State Department, unspecified work for a couple of international businesses (unnamed), and presently part-time consulting work (also unspecified).

He let her talk through several email exchanges and experienced a familiar feeling from their high school days of serving as an audience for a one person show. Then abruptly she switched gears. "So, how are you?"

she asked. "What's happening in your life?" The overture was one of those unexpected breezes that tickles you awake, reveals how stifling the air is around you, and hints of something you have unwittingly let slip away.

They had been sweethearts at Oneonta High School in Layton, back in the late '50s, early '60s, right after he, named Hamlet Horatio Sinclair by his literary parents, got the nickname "Ace" for striking out a blind kid in a summer-league baseball game.

The kid's dad stood behind the home plate umpire and yelled a number at the kid for how high the pitch was coming: *one*, *two*, *three* (feet), etc., and *zero* for a no-swing ball, and *now!* for when to cut loose. Ace got the kid on a full count. It was one of his few strikeouts.

"You some kind of ace!" his good-ole-boy coach said when Ace walked back to the dugout, then gave him a teasing push with his meaty fist. The name stuck with teammates, classmates, eventually everybody except his family. Ace felt a little guilty about the strike-out until the blind kid, Felix White, got into Princeton on a full scholarship and Ace barely made the waiting list.

At the time, J'nelle said she liked the nickname. He wondered sometimes whether she was teasing too— about how good she thought he was at making out, or maybe at how not-so-good. After he left his old haunts for college and law school in Chapel Hill and became a lawyer in Raleigh, the name came in handy: "ace in the courtroom." Nice ring to it, and certainly better than Ham or Horatio. And most of the time, he earned it.

5

He and J'nelle had been each other's first true love. They parted ways when she graduated a year ahead of him and went away to college. Basically, she just moved on. It knocked him for a loop, but he eventually staggered free of his teenage trance and into the fluorescent-lit certainty that all the world lay before him and all he had to do was reach out and grab his dreams as they drifted his way.

He shies from that image of himself as a loopy, out-of-it kid every time he senses it sauntering toward him around a corner. He takes a sip of Scotch. Beyond the dunes, waves land with a slow, muffled thunder.

So that had been it with him and J'nelle until his fiftieth Oneonta High reunion eight years ago. She attended because of all the friends she had in his class. He was in a daze then too: it was the first time he'd gone anywhere since Pam died. And there J'nelle was, standing with Seth and some other people across a lawn at the reunion picnic. He did not expect her to be there—she had not been on the list of possible attendees—and at first glance, from a side angle, he assumed it was someone else. But something about the way her wine glass swung between her thumb and index finger between sips and the way her hair moved when she turned her head told him it could be no one else. She had on a sundress that revealed the top half of her back. The lean muscles of the champion swimmer she'd been still lay on her shoulders, and when she raised her arm to drink, the ridge of her shoulder blade slipped smoothly under her lightly tanned skin.

Sixty-seven, sixty-eight years old. Jesus. The memories came flooding back of those times in high school when she wore a swimsuit or evening dress or when her blouse was unbuttoned and her bra undone in the back seat of his '55 Ford, his hands nervously searching, sometimes racing over her, his breath sucked and held, his brain whirling in wonder at the bounty coming his way.

At the reunion, he tried to bring the feeling of her skin and flesh back to his fingertips, but an ache came instead, not to his fingertips, but to his chest. The longing in it measured every millimeter of distance between him and that sunlit back across the reunion lawn.

And then a couple of years later, he heard about Seth's disappearance and sent the email of condolence. It took her some months to respond. That began a sporadic email conversation about nothing much and veered into questions of loss and how to deal with it and then into the nature of sadness. An intimation of mutuality crept in that caught him by surprise. It was like awakening in a dark room, hearing a match strike, and watching familiar fingers hold it to a candle. Their exchanges began to tiptoe as if they each sensed the presence of things still lost in the shadows. He found it strange that talking about grief and sadness could morph into such feelings of joy when he opened his email account and saw a new message from her.

Maybe she sensed his eagerness, and it scared her. Maybe she had enough grief of her own and decided she did not need to hear about his. Anyway, her responses became less frequent until finally they stopped. She was moving on. Again.

He went back to living the myth of himself as an old widowed lawyer nursing what was left of his life.

That had been six years ago, and now this latest, out-of-the-blue overture, and he was tiptoeing again. He answered politely, trying not to overdo things, all the while asking himself, *Overdo what?* until it became clear that it was not the glimpse of J'nelle's bare back at the reunion that affected him so much; it was the awakened memories of their long-lost past, and the sense that there were things unsaid, unresolved. The sensation was ghostlike, came and went, darting in and out of shadows, but quickly and with such dexterity that it seemed startlingly alive.

Old dreams, old memories, all gone, he had cautioned himself, and steered the email conversation back to catch-up mode. She had a daughter named Anna, about whom she did not seem to want to say much. She was downsizing her life. She had just sold her lake house in Maine, letting go of the last property she and Seth had bought together.

"Sorry you had to let it go," he wrote. "That seems to be the name of the game now. I'm in constant turmoil over what to do about my old family beach house on the North Carolina coast."

She had heard about his beach house in high school, but never visited it, and wanted to know about its history, his grandfather's vision for it, its architectural design. The house was one story, he told her, cypress

8

clapboard, white with green shutters, wraparound porches, and front steps that split into two flights on their way down—was all he could tell her.

"Low Country," she said.

"Pam and I added a deck on top of the roof to give us a better view."

"What would your grandfather think of that?"

"About the same thing he would think of a profanity at the dinner table. Anyway, you're welcome to use the house anytime you like, though I'm guessing it's a bit below what you are used to."

She let the subject drop until several emails later when he made the offer again, and out of politeness, he assumed, she asked more about it.

"Pomeiooc Island," he wrote, "maybe a bit too far south for you, now that you've become a sophisticated Yankee. Nothing fancy. Near what used to be an old fishing town, a bit back from the beach, window AC units that work off and on, so I go mostly in the winter and fall."

"It matches how I remember you."

"Like an old house?"

"No, I mean the 'nothing fancy' part and, 'a bit back from the beach'—authentic with a touch of shyness. Good place to retreat."

"Yeah, if you like peace and quiet and don't need a good restaurant."

"I don't need a good restaurant. And I like peace and quiet."

"That's funny. I don't remember you as a peace-and-quiet sort of person."

"Maybe you just didn't notice."

There was always a feeling when he was with her in high school—especially when they were alone—of another J'nelle inside her he could not see. He recalled a time when she sat across the car seat from him at a carhop drive-in in downtown Layton, a faraway look in her eyes. One of those sad, dreamy songs was on the radio—Buddy Holly's "It Doesn't Matter Anymore" or Roy Orbison's "Only the Lonely." Without looking at him, she said, "Take me home!" just like that. And he tried to move close, and she said, "No! Now, please!"

So he took her home, and he drove away with the feeling that a mystery, still in the shape of her, sat next to him in the car.

As the emails continued, he noticed in his voice a tone he didn't like, from those high school days, long ago. It wasn't desperation, but there was a running-to-catch-up quality about it in which his upper body seemed to lean dangerously forward of his feet. He thought he was done with it.

In early September, a few months after their latest email correspondence began, she flew to Europe for three weeks to do some consulting work in Paris and a cruise around the Iberian Peninsula. She went silent, and the silence haunted the empty spaces around him. His thoughts began to email amongst themselves: Was she meeting some guy in Paris? Was she alone on the cruise? It was none of his business, and why did he care? His brain composed fictional emails to her that came in sudden bursts. He scoffed at them, then caught himself revising furiously. Those old memories of dances, kisses, shadowy parking lots, and unbuttoned blouses rose in his dreams like red-winged blackbirds whirring out of a reed-choked marsh—their bright red and yellow epaulets flashing against their own blackness and a wintery sky that seemed to be his life.

In his sleep, he ached to reach for them, but he could not make his arms move.

After such a dream, he would awake and lie in the darkness—his fists clenched under the sheet, a calf twitching to cramp, and stare at the ceiling lit by the aquamarine numbers on his clock radio. This was crazy—these imaginary, compulsively worked-over emails, these seductive dreams that dragged him out of his settled past and across the tramped-over landscape of his life. The woman he had been emailing was not the girl who stirred those dreams. She wasn't even the older woman whose smooth muscled back he'd admired at the reunion eight years before. He had no idea who she was. He did not even know whether the details she had revealed in her emails were true or just what she wanted him to hear.

He was too old for this bullshit, and by God, he would cut it out: stop the emails, stop the whole deluded thing. If she contacted him after her return from Europe, well, he'd decide then what to do. But for sure he was going to put some brakes on it, slow it down, way down. And then, a quiet exit.

And he had been absolutely sure of that until the day he'd met with his doctor, Don Pearlman, about the battery of tests Pearlman suggested to help diagnose those tremors in his arms and weakness and muscle cramps in his legs. EMG, NCS, MRI, as if the acronyms could somehow hide what the tests were intended to find.

Pearlman leaned back against the examining table, arms crossed, and looked down at him, seated in the ass-grinding, vinyl-coated chair bought by whatever sadist buys doctors' office furniture. Ah, yes, and that ever-present stethoscope, a black noose down the front of Pearlman's white smock.

"I'll have Rob at the front desk call Carolina Radiology Center and schedule a date for you," Pearlman said. "We can probably get you in next week and have the results shortly thereafter."

"What do you think it is?"

"Dunno, buddy. Just have to wait and see."

"You've got a pretty good idea though, don't you?"

"There are at least a dozen possibilities, including nothing—that is to say, that 'nothing' we refer to as advancing maturity. Let's wait till all the evidence is in— isn't that what you lawyers say?"

"But if you had to bet."

"Ace, listen to what I'm saying. This is not a betting business. It's a test-and-wait-and-see business. Then if needed, test some more."

He rested a hand on Ace's shoulder. "Stay cool, don't push things and don't rush to judgment. We'll set up the tests. Meanwhile, do something—get out of town to that old place you've got at the beach. We'll try to get you a slot next week and give you a call."

By the time Ace got home, his landline answering machine flashed red with a message from the radiology center saying he was scheduled to appear in three weeks for a battery of tests that the scheduler ran through so hurriedly he could not pick them up. He started to hit the play-back button, then changed his mind and hit the erase button instead.

Two glasses of wine that night with supper, then a couple fingers of Oban to nurse through the first six innings of a listless outing by the Sox in Fenway until the rain blew in and they brought the tarps out. He pressed the mute button and watched the ground crews at work until the network switched to a playoff game on the West Coast between the Giants and Dodgers. Back in the old days, they were both New York teams—back when he was a kid, back when he was a high school kid and dating J'nelle, or the person he thought he knew as J'nelle.

It was when he got up from the TV and went back to the kitchen counter to pour himself another Scotch that it hit him: this was the day J'nelle was to return to New York from Europe. He froze and stared down at the tumbler of amber liquid with its always mysterious, oily swirl. This was the real test: his first night alone after his session with Pearlman—was he going to go to bed, get drunk, or do something else? What, exactly? He sloshed in a little more Scotch and pulled out his laptop.

"How was the trip?" he typed. "Please drop a line when you get a chance." His fingers froze in mid-air. No, not quite right: drop the "please." And maybe, "when you feel like it" instead of "when you get a chance," or maybe even better: "when you've recovered from your trip."

He swigged a gulp of Scotch.

"Fuck it!" he said and hit "send."

Silence for two days, then a short note: "I'm still a bit jet-lagged. More later when I'm on my feet."

"Take your time," he replied, then announced, "I'm probably headed to my beach house next week to do some reflecting on things," a phrase he almost gagged on—that running-to-catch-up tone again, that anticipation of a tumble. He hated new age bullshit! But he was even more fed up with his own jacking around, and tacked on another sentence at the end that caught him even more by surprise: "Let me know if you'd be interested in talking by phone."

"Sure," she replied the next day. "Just give me some advance notice on when you might call."

He suggested three possible evenings. She picked the last one. When the time finally came, he fortified himself with another round of wine and Scotch and fought to aim the fat tip of his index finger at the tiny keys on his cell phone in spite of that familiar tremor that he now called the Pearlman Shake.

"Hey," she said, "I was a little doubtful you'd call. Good to hear your voice."

"Good to hear yours," he said. "So, how was the trip?"

In high school she had something close to a photographic memory that sucked up every detail, and when she got excited about something, those details came pouring out, as they did on the phone call. She gave him the tour: Paris restaurants and museums—her favorite, the Musée d'Orsay, and a new discovery, the Musée du quai Branly, with its works from Africa, Asia, and the Americas. Then on to Barcelona and the cruise ship—some Norwegian line—and its stops at Valencia, Gibraltar, Lisbon, etc., etc., along the Spanish and Portuguese coasts. Her voice had the same chameleon-like quality of the young J'nelle's voice that hopscotched back and forth from light to shadow, except that now the tone had a rawness about it, as if chafed by age.

He put his phone on speaker and treaded water in a thickening broth of French, Spanish, and Portuguese names and places and restaurant menus. Could this stranger, this globe-trotting woman, whose voice buzzed out at him from that nest of microchips and plastic resting in his palm, be a real-life link to those red-winged blackbirds flashing through his dreams? From somewhere deep in the space-age magic of the phone, the word "folly" flashed out at him.

He grabbed at his first chance to interrupt.

"Sounds terrific. Do you do these cruises all by yourself?"

"Usually."

"I'm impressed."

Pause. Then another shift in tone, a quick step back to that image of her across the car seat from him in high school. *Take me home, please.*

"I've been taking care of myself for years," she said.

He recalled a moment in high school when he was a second-string running back and got called into the

15

state championship game when the star got his bell rung. On Ace's first carry, the quarterback jammed a handoff into his gut. The body parts he had trained so hard to make ready—arms, wrists, and hands—turned to rubber as if they had been waiting for this moment to betray him. He bobbled the ball and lunged forward, reaching, grabbing, even yelling at it, and he can still feel its leathery weight tumble off the tips of his fingers.

"Sure," he said into the sky blue face of his iPhone, "of course you have."

He did not hear her sigh, but he sensed it.

"So," she said, "you're about to take your own trip."

"I am?"

"To your beach house—didn't you say?"

"Oh that—yeah, in a few days. I need to get away. It just sits there waiting."

"Peace and quiet."

"Yeah, peace and quiet."

And once again, that reaching, grabbing feeling as the football slipped away. And why in the fuck couldn't he stop himself?

"You know," he said, "you are welcome to use it whenever."

"Thanks."

The ball, beyond reach now, off the tips of his fingers, bouncing on the ground toward a diving scrum of players just before his nose and face guard plow into the dirt.

"I mean, you are welcome to come down. I'll be there for the last part of the week and through the weekend."

On her end, he heard a small tap or click, a pen perhaps tapping a desk or table, a glass being set on a counter. God forbid, a remote.

"You mean, come down while you're there?"

"Well yes, if you'd like to."

More silence, then again the tap, tap.

"Ace, I'm not sure that's a good idea?"

"I've pretty much quit worrying about what's a good idea."

For a couple of seconds after that blown hand-off in high school, he lay on his back and stared up at the nighttime sky, hazed over with the stadium lights' yellow glow, and felt a strange peace with himself, maybe with everything. That had been his chance for gridiron glory, and there he was, there was no going back to do it over. And so the future, well, it would have to be whatever it would have to be.

"I guess I'm surprised, to say the least," she said, "and I appreciate the offer…"

"Nothing fancy," he said, "a weekend maybe, or a few days. It's not that hard to get to. I'm flexible. I can pick you up at the Raleigh airport, and we can drive down together."

Silence.

"You know, just catch up, get reacquainted. I don't want to scare you."

More silence.

"J'nelle—I'm too old for seduction, and it never worked with you anyway. We can just hang out and— what's that line from the Springsteen song?—'talk about the old times.' I assure you, my intentions are honorable."

She chuckled. "You haven't turned into one of those creepy old men who prey on helpless old ladies?"

"One thing I'm still sure of: you are not helpless."

"OK. Look, let me think about this."

"Email me or give me a call. I'll do all the planning."

He knew that whatever her answer, it would come by email and not by phone. And maybe it would not come by either, or by UPS or snail mail or Morse code. And if so, that would be the end of it.

"Sorry I'm so hesitant about this," she wrote. "Life has been fairly confusing lately, and I'm a bit unsettled. I can come, but not until the weekend. I've got to rearrange some things on this end, make airline reservations, and line up a rental car."

"I'll pay for all of that," he said.

"Not on your life."

And so here he is on his roof deck on this particular night, watching the stream of headlights.

He removes his baseball cap and lets a breeze off the sound whip the ragged locks of whitening hair that tickle his neck just above his collar top. The stream of car lights crossing the inlet bridge has thinned. The cars move toward him as solitary, slow-moving beacons. Stars are out, showing themselves in that slow, barely noticed way that also seems sudden, and form their ancient patterns in the sky. He thinks of Matthew Arnold's poem,

"Dover Beach"—the calm sea, the moon lying fair upon the straits, "Come to the window, sweet is the night-air!"

When Pam was alive, she would point out the constellations to him from this very deck, Taurus, Orion, the two Ursas, she knew them all. She was an artist, and something about the patterns of light spoke to her artistic spirit. They were so clear to her, but even as he tried to follow where she was pointing, he had a hard time making them out, and one night it came to him that his problem was not his weaker eyesight but the lack of an instinct. Pam had an internal sextant, a magical tool of her artistic nature that saw the pinpoints of light even before they blinked in the purple darkness. And when she tried to show him what she saw, he always felt small and was unsure how much of that was due to the vastness of the heavens and the magic they offered and how much of it was because of her natural affinity with it all. It was the same with birds and seashells and butterflies and mushrooms. Her inbred knack for knowing them deepened and brightened with age, even as the ruddy hue of her skin, framed by her gray, bowl-cut hair, paled toward the whiteness of death.

She had the same bowl cut as a kid. He saw it in a picture of her on a bureau in her parents' house. Dressed in khaki pants and high boots that looked way too big, she had just returned from a deer hunt with her father. The way she stood next to him, held onto his paw-like hand, and looked up at him without really looking—you could almost smell the woods on them and picture the scene: Pam trailing behind among giant hardwoods on

the way to their deer stand, searching for fall wildflow-
ers and mushrooms. *Come on, Pam. Keep your eyes in front of
you and watch where you point that gun.*

She tried to take him hunting once when she was
pregnant with their first child, Eli, and he trailed behind her until he stopped in his tracks and said, "I don't
want to do this."

She turned and gave him a hug, that same bowl cut
pressed against his cheek.

"I don't want to anymore either," she said. "Let's
watch birds."

They walked back to the car and traded guns for binoculars.

Their life together was chock-full, like she was, and
then he sat and watched as the morphine dripped in
and she faded and faded, until somewhere, in a quiet
known only to her, she was gone.

He leans forward, elbows on his knees, and turns
his empty whiskey glass slowly in his hands. His limbs
feel fragile and wobbly with his grief. Beneath him the
boards of the deck blur in the light of the moon. She is
out there somewhere—in the wooded darkness off the
side of the deck, up there in the starry sky. Watching?
No. Waiting? No, just there. What does she think of this
mess he has gotten himself into?

"Ace, have you thought this through? Be careful, you
could get hurt."

Hopeless romantic, she once called him. "Beneath it
all—trial lawyer, war vet, make-believe hard ass—that's
what you are."

Beneath him he feels the house begin to stir. Always in a full moon, the ghosts are restless. Pam sensed them the first time she came to the house after they were married. Two old maid aunts of his lived in the house for years and died here, as did a widowed uncle, and an infant child of a distant cousin, bitten in the face by a water moccasin. Maybe they anticipate J'nelle's coming, the invasion by a strange woman. They were all hardcore Presbyterians and would not approve of unchaperoned cohabitation, even for a weekend. And how about the other spirits, the ones who hover in the woods between the house and the main road, guarding the graves of the ancient ones who lived here long before the whites came? Something tells him they know all about J'nelle, and about him as well, knew about this visit even before that last reunion. For them, the invasion came long ago.

He gets to his feet, turns his back on the water, sky, and night sounds, and descends the steps to the front porch and the door that leads to the main room, where he will wash out his glass, put up the bottle, and go to bed. That rocking cradle. That lonely, gray darkness of sleep.

But tonight the cradle does not rock. Instead, the dreams come—the house dream first, in which he wanders through a multistory house of endless rooms and torturous corridors, searching for something he cannot identify but which seems critically important. He keeps hoping that Pam will come to help him search, but she never shows, and the dream ends with a sudden, unexpected exit into nowhere.

And the jungle dream, in which he is back in Vietnam, and the war is still going on, except that he is not a young soldier, but old like he is now. Crack North Vietnamese units are nearby; rockets, artillery shells, and mortars whack into the jungle. The North Vietnamese attack through the wire and run through the American camp, throwing grenades and firing AK-47s. He tries frantically to get the attention of his superior—some blank-faced, empty-brained martinet who brought him there from the States—but the officer will not listen. And then the searching feeling returns, just as in the other dream about the house, and there is nothing to find, and this time there is no exit.

Friday morning

He wakes late, having once again forgotten to set an alarm, sits on the edge of the bed, and fumbles at the message app on his cell phone. A slight headache from the night before. Maybe a little too much Scotch on the upper deck as he weaved his way down memory lane.

The app is there, exactly where it's supposed to be, but the thumbs are not quite up to the job. He switches to his index finger, and blink!—there it is, an 8:25 a.m. message from J'nelle: "Just landed in Raleigh. See you soon."

Damn, he's been so distracted chasing memories and tracing the twisted path of how her plan to visit came about, he hasn't thought through the details, like how long it takes to fly from La Guardia to RDU, pick up the rental car, and head east toward the island. A weekend, light traffic, she could be at his house, looking up at him from the bottom of his back-porch steps, in a little over three hours.

He braces his fists on the mattress and pushes himself to his feet. A slight tremor in his right wrist migrates to his knuckles and fingers. But he will be OK—the next steps are memorized: walk to the toilet, stand holding his dick for however long it takes, get in the

23

shower, and lower the water temp until he finally wakes up—a trick Pam suggested because, she said, she was tired of talking to a zombie every morning.

All is on track until he steps from the shower, grabs the towel, and catches a glimpse of himself in the mirror above the line of prescription pill bottles he has trouble keeping straight. *Sweet Jesus,* he thinks, *that cannot be me!* Muscles vanish before his eyes, which themselves have a vanishing look as they stare back at him from their deepening sockets of purple. White hair leaps from his pate as if fleeing a condemned building.

He rummages through the drawer by the sink for his barber scissors. He cuts his hair every three months or so—he can't stand barber shops and places with names like "Fancy Cuts"—and he's a month overdue. But this morning, the first joint of his arthritic thumb will not fit through the hole on the scissors handle. He tries the scissors in his left hand until the tremor hits.

"Fuck it," he says and jams the scissors back in the drawer. He dresses and heads down the hallway to the main room to fix breakfast, walking straight and tall with that old military bearing he affects sometimes to remind him that once, long ago, he was, well, straight and tall. The feeling lasts until he steps into the main room and takes a look around. The house has not been cleaned in months except for his half-assed, lick-and-a-promise effort. He can smell it: dirt and dust everywhere, mold climbing the grouting in bathroom tiles, mouse droppings in the drawers and corners, that bat-like stink in unaired closets.

He puts on coffee, eats a quick breakfast, then vacuums, wipes, and dusts in a flurry that reminds him of an *I Love Lucy* episode in which Lucy scurries about with her hair wrapped in a scarf pushing a vacuum with one hand, wielding a dust mop, broom, and dustpan with the other—on her face that scatterbrained, wild-eyed look of panic as she rushes to clean up some goofy mess she's made, before her husband Ricky comes home. All of this over a weekend visit from an old girlfriend—an old woman—he hasn't known for almost sixty years. For all he knows, her eyesight is so bad she can't even see the dirt. He tries to put the Lucy image out of his mind, but it keeps coming back, like a TV channel that pops back on every time you try to change it.

"To hell with it," he says.

He straightens from cleaning the shower in the guest bedroom, throws the brush under the counter, gives the toilet an extra flush, and looks at his watch. Nearly ten-thirty. He grabs wallet and car keys and clambers down the steps to his car, drawing a list in his head of the ingredients for fish stew, his specialty. He'll hit the fish market first, then on to the grocery store for vegetables, fruits, lettuce, and—oh yeah, toilet paper and probably a bunch of other stuff.

And maybe some bottled water?

He freezes with his hand on the car door handle. What about the storm? His house is on a well, and his generator is an old 7000-watt Briggs & Stratton. He hits the weather app on his cell phone: Freya has reclaimed her status as a Category 1 hurricane and has slid up the map to roughly the latitude of the Georgia-Florida line. Tracking lines spray all over the Southeast coast and northward out to sea. So, nothing to worry about yet, but he might as well grab some water just in case. And maybe fill up with gas. There'll probably be a run on that too.

The fish market yields grouper, shrimp, and clams, each with its special brand of stink, bagged in separate pockets of ice and slime. At the supermarket, he fights his way through a traffic jam of carts loaded with water, milk, bread, OJ, and canned goods in time to grab the last six gallons of water, then turns to face an empty cart pushed by a wild-eyed, underfed-looking woman, translucent skin stretched tight across the bones of her face, a snake tattoo slithering from the top of her tank top to under her chin. Two equally wild-eyed kids trail behind her, maybe three and five years old.

Her eyes are probably brown, but they seem black, as if he is staring into holes in the earth.

"Here," he says, and holds out one of the water jugs. "You take it—take 'em all. I can fill up the bathtub."

The woman and her kids watch as he unloads the water from his basket into hers, then they turn and walk away without a word of thanks. The kids look back at him over their shoulders, the younger one's thumb stuck deep into its mouth.

Drugs, he thinks. He saw it many times as a lawyer in Raleigh. Now meth has spread up and down the coast, with crime rising in its wake. He's been reading about it for years in the Raleigh paper, seeing the statistics.

So why is it just now occurring to him? The storm, maybe—people become desperate after a bad storm. And he won't be alone. He'll have a guest. Maybe he should be more careful, start locking the house.

He grabs a bunch of corsage-like flowers on his way to the check-out. Lavenders, yellows, pinks, and greens. Carnations, he guesses, but he thought they came only in red and white, at least they did in high school when he gave them to J'nelle for some dance or other. A thick ball of white pinned to her shoulder, glaring back at him when he got too close.

The day has warmed to an unseasonable seventy-plus degrees, and by the time he hauls the groceries and seafood up the steps and into the kitchen, he's sweating. He sticks the flowers in a vase on the dining room table and busies himself stowing the food, soaking the clams, and peeling the shrimp, between glances at his watch. Something about the flurry of his hands over bowls, sink, and counter tops seems more hurried than usual—that *I Love Lucy* feeling again. When he wrings out the wash rag in the sink, it's like wringing out a shrinking remnant of himself.

It is not that wild man he saw in the mirror earlier that worries him. It is the possibility, perhaps the likelihood, that to everybody but himself, he is boring. The round-cheeked checkout clerk in the grocery store kept her mascara eyes on the groceries he fed her and never looked up at him as she scanned them.

"Good mornin', ju find everything?" (Zip, zip, zip)

"Yes," he answered. "Nice day."

"So far." (Zip, zip, zip)

He could have been a movie star, a drag queen, a blue-faced baboon. She didn't even glance up as he swiped his card.

He finds Pam's old binoculars, climbs to the upper deck, and stands at the railing to search the sky for whatever happens by. Beyond the breakers, gulls squawk and fight over a morsel that drops from their grasps into the water that sloshes like melted silver under a cloud-muted sun. In the far distance, the Crowbank Inlet Bridge is all concrete pilings and bleached cement as it slopes downward to join the gray asphalt road. The cars move over it in business-like progression. He thinks of lines from T.S. Eliot's *The Waste Land*: "A crowd flowed over London Bridge... I had not thought death had undone so many."

In a time long ago, he was part of that flow, the Raleigh version of it: off to work, grind out his days in office or court, back home at night to the father-husband thing, then off to bed, six hours, maybe seven, rise early, refuel with coffee, and head off into the next day. He liked it though, didn't he? Most of the time, some of the time. It's hard sometimes to remember.

He takes a seat in the rope-back hammock chair and rests the binoculars in his lap. A slight breeze. He fancies he can hear the endless purr of engines, way out there in the distance on the bridge, the bump of tires over strips of asphalt spacing the slabs of concrete. He's been here before, this feeling of being caught in a pause in time between what has gone before, or what he believes has gone before, and whatever is coming. Maybe it is a premonition of death. Maybe that's how it happens: there is a pause where everything stops, and this arrangement with J'nelle, this commitment to whatever disruption she will bring, is a way to keep things going, kick-start his way out of the pause.

The knock on the back door vaults him from the chair, down the stairs to the front porch, and into the house. Once there, he slows his steps to an easy pace across the main room toward the back entranceway door where she is framed in the full-length glass. She is taller and thinner than he remembers, especially compared to his memory of that bare back above the top of her sun dress. Maybe over the years he unconsciously enhanced that memory, air-brushed it with other memories of Esther Williams in her swimsuit, or Betty Grable, or that new actress, what's-her-name—he can never remember.

A wild spray of hair with hints of red and gold fading to white brushes her shoulders. There is something fraught about it, as if it's a part of her she's been at war with for years but has finally given up trying to control. And lurking in it, no doubt, like a sweet predator, is that hint of shampoo that often lurks in women's hair. Silver earrings flash from just beneath the spray and send a wind-burned tint along the gaunt ridges of her nose and high cheekbones. Prominent eyebrows shadow blue-green eyes, traced with flecks of gold that make them seem lightning-struck. It's all there, just as it was before—the brightness, the rawness, the eagerness, the hesitation, right down to the slightly worried smile—only more so, and it strikes him as an astonishing reduction of the flush of her youth to the burned-in beauty of age.

The doorknob is corroded from the salty air. He twists away at it until it finally gives, then throws the door open—and freezes.

"Hey," she says.

The blue-green eyes brighten; her smile holds its tension in the creases at the top and corners of her lips.

A sigh, a slight shrug of her angular shoulders.

"Your directions were perfect. I didn't have to listen to that obnoxious voice on the rental car GPS, telling me where to turn."

He takes a step back, as if to distance himself from a glaring light that has just flashed on in a dark room.

"Great," he says, "that's really great. Glad they worked."

Her carry-on, an expensive-looking one, stuffed and bulging, sits next to her on the porch. Tied to its handle to help her ID it in the bag carousel is a fluff of sand-colored knitting yarn that almost matches her hair. Her earrings are round and intricately designed. They swivel slowly in the quiet hum of her body's static energy. She never wore anything like that when he knew her, just a charm bracelet with girl stuff on it.

"You look great," he says. "It's really great of you to come. I'll get that." He reaches for the carry-on and jerks the bag over the sill and into the house, then freezes again. The bedroom—he hadn't thought about having to show her her bedroom, but it is the next logical step.

"Thanks," she says. The smile relaxes a bit; the eyes twinkle.

"OK if I come in?"

"Oh! Yeah, sure." He shuffles backwards with the bag. "Sorry. Maybe I'm a bit nervous."

She steps into the house and glances around. "Yeah, me too."

"So," he says, "this way," and starts toward the guest bedroom, rolling the carry-on behind him across the heart-of-pine floor. The wheels rumble like the wheels of an ancient ox-cart or maybe a hearse or maybe one of those carts they used in the old days to haul people to the gallows. She feels it too, he can tell, as if the rumble comes from long ago, and the bag is a crypt of squeaky, bat-like memories waiting for him to hit a bump so the lid can fly open.

He stops at the guest-bedroom door and stands aside for her to peer in. "I hope this is OK."

"It's nice," she says, gazing about at what she can see of the house's interior. "I like it—the house. It makes being here more than just being at the beach."

"Yeah—good way to put it."

"It reminds me of my grandmother's place in Florida, where my family used to go for Christmas."

Always family with her—in the old days, that got in the way a lot.

"Yeah, it stirs up memories for me too, but sometimes I don't think the house is worth it—it's too much

31

trouble to keep up."

"I know; I owned an old house once. They can be a real pain in the ass."

Ah, yes—the two sides of the old J'nelle. When they first met in high school, she was the non-curser, the straight-A student whose face beamed from the choir stall into the sunlit vault of their church as she stole shy glances at him, the altar boy. Then toward the end of her senior year, especially late in the evenings, another J'nelle emerged. She smoked cigarettes, drank beer, and cursed, and led them into escapades he'd have never dreamed up himself, like the night they drove to Birmingham to spy on a Klan rally, or the morning of her last day in school when she talked him into skipping class, buying some beer, and sneaking off to a secret spot they knew by the river. He called this other version of her Midnight J'nelle, and that version scared him a little. She's the one who, without actually saying it, kept bringing up the year's difference in their ages. She's the one who gave him the feeling of being left behind.

"And there's the bathroom." He gestures toward a door opening off the bedroom to reveal a toilet and part of the shower.

Christ, what else could it be!

"Thanks. Give me a minute, I want to change out of this." She gestures toward her tan, pressed slacks and open-toed shoes.

Should he offer a drink, a glass of water first? He should have put some in her room, like they do in B&Bs and nice hotels. Pam would have done that.

"If that's OK?" she says.

"Sure."

She takes the carry-on handle from him with a quick brush of flesh—the student council president from days of yore, striding into the high school from the parking lot with a load of books, crammed with perfectly done homework, wrapped in her long, swimmer's arms.

He waits in the kitchen area of the great room with his palms pressed flat on the counter and looks about without seeing anything, but feeling the urgent presence of the house around him—the exposed beams where he and Pam had the ceiling removed and the once nice but now old furniture and curtains and lamps and throw rugs with their vacuum-cleaner-chewed corners and edges.

A slight gulp of saliva, a nervous twitter in his forearm.

Something in him has weakened since last night when he sat on the deck and watched the lights. The dreams maybe. The dreams never help.

He hears the toilet flush and waits in the familiar no-man's-land he recalls from high school, long moments spent slouched against walls across the hall from a ladies' room—at movie theaters and ball games. The minutes swelled into fathoms like the ocean now before him. And then she would emerge and smile, and the hallway, full of milling, murmuring people, would suddenly have a center moving toward him like the star of a play had walked onstage. She'd say something like, "Don't be such a grouch," as if waiting on her was part of his job and he might as well get used to it, because someday it would become a fact of life.

The bedroom door shuts, and she emerges from the hall and walks toward him. He notices—or perhaps allows himself to see for the first time—her shape in a cotton, ankle-length wraparound skirt. The saucy bounce of old is gone. Now she glides like Venus on the water or King Arthur's Lady of the Lake, with an airy quietness that seems almost solemn. A loose blouse of linen or something similar is tied at the waist, and on her long, slender wrist, below one of the floppy sleeves, is one of those flat-faced Apple watches or something similar with a pitch black dial and mesh stainless-steel band. A stack of loose bracelets circles the other wrist, hooped and silver, except for one of hammered copper that he recognizes, from one of his and Pam's trips, as African.

She offers a crisp smile, as if officially declaring her arrival. "Where's the ocean?" she says. "After a morning in cars and airports, I could use some fresh air."

"Follow me."

He leads her to the upper deck. She walks past him to the railing and takes a deep breath.

"It feels so good to be here," she says. She turns to face him and rests her backside against the railing. "I can see why you love this place."

"How about a proper welcome?" he says, pushing through his uncertainty to step forward and open his arms. She responds tentatively, circling her arms lightly about his waist only after he has encircled her in his. Her body does not feel weak, but lighter, thinner and less tensile, the eager physicality gone and in its place a nervous hesitation, like a sparrow perched to fly. He wonders what his body feels like to her: his soft middle, growing softer year-by-year; his slack, toneless arms; the roll of extra flesh about his waist where her arms rest, barely touching.

She lets go, rests against the railing, and throws her head back.

"I love this early fall weather! How often do you come here?"

As they stand and stare out at the corrugated surface of the sea, the small talk begins: the story of the house and the five acres around it; how by the process of attrition, uncles and aunts, father, older sibling, the place came to be his.

"Old places have an aura," she says at least twice as he answers her questions about the house's structure, the old beams and floors, the slatted shutters and dry-stack, hand-chipped stone in the front porch steps. With each tidbit of the house's history, with each recitation of structural detail, he can feel the tone in his voice go flatter.

She brushes a breeze-loosened lock from her forehead. "You don't sound very enthusiastic about all of this."

Out beyond the dunes, gulls squawk over slow-moving swells that slosh with metronomic regularity on the beach.

"It's doomed."

"Why?"

"The ocean," he says, "is growing very hungry."

Her gaze rests coolly on the side of his face.

"You know," he says, "global warming, the rising sea level."

"Well, sooner or later, yes. But not for a while, at least. Not in our lifetimes."

He leans forward, elbows resting on the railing. "There's a storm brewing out there right now that could do it. The next nor'easter could do it. The whole island is doomed."

She turns back to face the sea. The breeze lifts her hair, wing-like, off her shoulders, ruffles her loose blouse, and presses it against her upper body. There is a good foot between them, but what would it be like now, after all these years, to feel the press of her shoulder against his?

"We grew up," she says, "with the end of the world hanging over us, remember? I used to have nightmares over those images of mushroom clouds they kept throwing at us. It's kind of like that now, except now I feel responsible."

"For the end of the world?"

"Don't you? I could have reduced my carbon footprint a little over the years—smaller house, smaller car, bought less of everything, instead of bingeing on life. It's like an habitual sin." She pauses and takes a deep breath. "Against the universe, no less."

There it is, he thinks, *the class president side of her who watched her footprints very carefully*.

"As I recall," he says, "you were always big on

sin—guarding against it, that is—but not so big on guilt."

He has tip-toed so carefully until now, hasn't he, but there is that throat-tightening feeling of having stepped over an edge.

She drops her words on him slowly, one-by-one, like weights. "What the hell does that mean?"

"When we did something forbidden, like the night we drove across the state line to Meridian to the air force base and bought that fifth of gin that tasted like formaldehyde, or the day we slipped off into the woods from that church picnic to make out, you saw them as big steps over the line, but once we'd done them, you didn't seem to worry about it."

She turns and looks him straight in the eye. "You may not have seen everything."

He is suddenly conscious of the uneven boards beneath his feet, an uneasiness in his legs, the hint of a tremor up his calf to behind his knee.

"Maybe I got it wrong," he says. "I got a lot of things wrong back then."

Far out over the water, an osprey that for some reason has not yet migrated south for the winter, plunges straight down onto a fish, and there is that split second of wonder at how a bird that descends from the sky that fast and hits the water that hard can ever rise, until the wings spread and the bird slowly rises with the fish gripped in its talons, adjusted to face its line of flight.

Friday afternoon

S he stands across from him at the island counter in the kitchen and sips her beer while he puts together sliced turkey and cheese sandwiches, adds dill pickles to the plates, and pulls open a bag of chips. He can feel her eyes on him and on the tremor in his hand as he lowers the serrated knife blade to cut the sandwiches. *Stop, damnit!* he says to himself, but the shake continues until the blade bites into the bread.

She plies him with questions about his life as a lawyer. He sums it up as mostly done, so she probes for details all the way back to his days in law school—cases, clients, firms, the decision to go to law school in the first place, which really began with the decision to bail out on his English Lit PhD more than halfway through.

It was a tortuous path that seems even more so in the telling, almost as if it is the story of the life of a stranger. He finds himself hedging, cutting answers short, dodging completely the two years in the army after he dropped out of grad school, and he dodges as well the Pam part, the way her cozy presence and smooth energy helped him get the Vietnam monkey off his back and take the next step to law school and then to whatever he finally became, which somehow feels abandoned by who he is now.

38

Her questions keep coming through lunch and an impromptu tour she begins of the house. He can hear in his answers that touch of testiness he fought so hard to keep out of his voice during his days in court. When it got loose, it was his worst enemy.

She goes quiet as she looks over the antique relics in the main room, running her hands lovingly over the old surfaces. It irritates him, he's not sure why. They walk down the hall toward his study and the other bedrooms. At the door to the master bedroom, she touches his elbow.

"Why don't we leave the rest of this for later? I'd like to see the beach."

They don light jackets and walk across the sunlit yard to the pathway through the dunes. The tide is low, the beach wide and open. They remove their shoes and walk near the water, where the waves wash over their feet and wet the bottom of her skirt. Ahead of them, sanderlings scurry about to take small crustaceans in the wake of retreating waves. Willets, plovers, and the occasional oystercatcher search for targets of opportunity. The beach is deserted except for them and the birds and a young woman in a pink windbreaker, who walks ahead of them and pauses occasionally to raise her binoculars and study the birds. Her black hair is chopped and short, like Pam's used to be. It hangs about her head like a cowl.

"So," he says, "you dropped out of Hollins for the Peace Corps, then went back to get your degree, then on to grad school at UVA, then marriage and the usual trials of parenthood with your daughter, Anna, and what else—life happily ever after?"

She smiles. "It wasn't quite that simple."

"Never is," he says, "but you've had an impressive career—Peace Corps, State Department, spreader of good works, international expert of some kind—as yet unexplained—still zipping off to Paris and Spain, much of that time raising a kid. That sounds like quite a life to me."

They walk in the silence left by the seething hiss of retreating waves. She hugs her arms to her chest like the young woman walking ahead of them, pressing her unbuttoned jacket closed. The breeze blows her hair across her face in what seems a peekaboo with her own thoughts.

"I need to tell you something," she says.

"Sure."

She steps ahead and plants herself to face him. So many variations in those tightly pressed lips, and this version he remembers but cannot put a name to.

"You may not like it," she says.

"J'nelle, I spent my life as a lawyer learning to handle things I didn't like."

She turns and resumes walking, her arms still pressed about her.

"I did join the Peace Corps, but the real reason I left Hollins was to have an abortion.

An unnamed dread taps his shoulder. The child was not his; he knows that for sure because when she was with him, they were too goody-two-shoes to make it all

40

the way. But he also knows that the next step in their conversation will take him deep into the shadow of the unknown.

"Mason Morrel," she says.

He stops. After a few steps, she does as well, with her back to him.

"Mason Morrel," he says, "our English teacher?"

Morrel, a dark-haired, light-footed athletic guy in his mid-twenties, was one of Ace's favorite teachers. There was a spontaneous excitement about him that infected his students and ignited their enthusiasm for learning into a joy that seemed to infect Morrel himself. Ace and other guys in Morrel's classes thought of him as both a role model and buddy.

"But how could that be?" Ace says, "I mean, when did it happen—when we were still in high school?"

"*It* happened after I left for college. He drove up to see me a couple of weekends."

"Just out of the blue?"

"The thing between us began before that, at the end of my senior year."

The thing between us.

"He was married," Ace says, "wasn't he?"

"Yes, he was married."

He remembers seeing her and Mason Morrel together at the far end of a hallway one rainy day in high school, silhouetted against a large, dirt-stained window. Mason was tall, an ex-basketball player, and she held her books to her chest and looked up at him. As Ace drew near, Mason leaned toward her, very close, and whispered something, then walked away. And she stood there, holding her books with her head down.

Morrel must have known Ace and J'nelle were a couple; everyone did. And when Ace had him as a teacher in senior English the next year, Morrel was on the road to visit J'nelle at Hollins.

Ace opens his mouth to speak, but only a rush of breath comes out.

She resumes walking up the beach. He follows.

"So," he says, fighting a sudden choke in his voice, "you started with Mason while we were still, supposedly, going together."

Again she does not respond.

"And all through the summer after you graduated, before you went off to college?"

His rising voice seems to levitate him, buoy him on the wind.

"You were out west, remember," she says, "learning to be a mountain man or woodsman or whatever you went out there to do."

"And that makes it OK?"

She turns to face him.

"I'm not trying to make it OK, Ace."

"But I saw you that summer, after I came back from working in Yellowstone."

"Yes," she says, "we went out twice. I intended to tell you then things were over, but I just couldn't. It all seemed so sad."

She looks away from him, out over the water toward the inlet bridge.

The woman in the pink windbreaker has turned to stare at them, her binoculars held loosely at her side. Ace's eyes go to her, then to J'nelle, then back to the woman, who is not young at all, but as old as he and J'nelle. *What are you staring at?*, he thinks. *What do you see?*

He holds the woman's gaze until she turns and moves on, then he turns back to J'nelle, who resumes her walk away from him up the beach.

"I guess that explains why you quit writing me soon after you went off to Hollins."

J'nelle keeps walking, only more slowly, head bowed, shoulders hunched.

He has an image of himself his senior year, ripping open her letters at the mailbox at the end of his driveway and reading them right there, even in the rain as the drops smeared that graceful girlish script that reminded him of the way she felt in his arms when they danced to something rhythmic and slow. But there was no rhythm in her words, only the flat catalog of her days. The letters came less frequently, the weight of them grew lighter, the script seemed more hurried. Or was that just his imagination? By mid-November, they stopped, and he learned the vastness of silence for the first time. She didn't come home for Thanksgiving, and by the time Christmas holidays began, her parents had moved to Michigan. But it took till February, maybe even March, before he would admit that what they had was gone, just like that, as if a magnificent bird—one of those glistening, royal peacocks that look handcrafted—had lifted from the ground next to him and vanished into the sky.

"Well," he says, "I'll be damned."

She stops and turns to face him.

"I'm sorry, Ace, truly. I hate to shatter old dreams, but I've felt I owed you the truth for a long time, and I just couldn't accept your generous hospitality for a weekend without clearing the air. You were a wonderful guy, and you came into my life at just the right time. It's hard to imagine how I would have gotten through those last years of high school without you."

She stands with her arms folded, head tilted slightly forward, and studies his face. "You're upset, aren't you?"

"I always thought of you as the girl who was so perfect, so always in control."

She continues to study him.

"I guess," he says, "looking back, I probably built it up into something a lot more than it really was. I tended to do that back then."

She smiles a hesitant smile.

"Or maybe," he says, "I've done that in the years since."

"No," she says. "It was there. I'm not sure why I did what I did except my mind sort of burst its seams and left Layton before I did. I was so desperate to leave that whole scene behind: parents, rules, silly girlfriends, high school clothes, high school talk, all of it."

He shrugs. "Including me."

The smile vanishes. She turns her head and looks out over the rolling swells, her lips pressed but askew, the bottom one tugging slightly at the upper. This woman, this messenger from the past, holding up a severed head—his head.

She turns back to face him, takes a slow half-step forward, then stops.

"Ace, I don't know what else to say except that under that facade you saw of me having it all under control, I was insecure, self-centered, and sometimes—in a way and for reasons I still don't fully understand—devious, even to myself, especially to myself. It's hard for me to imagine myself as I was then."

He takes a few steps toward the ocean and stares out over the water. The breaking waves scurry across the sand, pushing their borders of foam. Above him, the gulls squawk louder and seem very close.

Her voice comes from behind him and sounds far away.

"I'd like to go back to the house," she says. "Will you come?"

"You go ahead. I think I'll walk a bit longer."

He walks past her down the beach as she follows him with her eyes. Ten paces on, he stops and turns. She is headed away from him down the beach toward the house, still hunched forward, arms wrapped about her.

"There's some red wine already open on the counter and a bottle of white in the fridge," he calls, "and the beer."

When she does not respond, he says a bit louder: "I didn't mean to overreact. It just caught me by surprise."

45

And to himself he whispers, "How could I let myself get so caught up in such a fucking dream?"

Friday evening

When he returns to the house, she is not in sight. Her bedroom door is closed. He takes a seat on the front porch and props his feet against the railing. Beyond a break in the dunes, the gray ocean lolls lazily in the dull afternoon sun. A slight chill is settling in. After ten minutes, he hears her footsteps behind him in the main room. She stops at the screen door.

"Do you want me to leave?" she asks. "I can find a motel until tomorrow, then head back."

"No, I'm fine. It was over fifty years ago."

He rises from the chair and heads past her into the house. "C'mon, let's make some supper. I'm working on a fish stew I've been perfecting for years. You cook?"

"As little as possible."

He pours wine in two of Pam's hand-painted glasses. She takes his instructions, chops celery and onions, minces garlic, and finishes peeling the shrimp. He fries andouille sausage in olive oil; adds the celery and onions, garlic, bay leaf, diced tomatoes, and tomato sauce to build the broth, finally adding a splash of dry white wine before dropping in the chunks of fish, clams, and shrimp; then puts together a small salad. They talk about kids—his son, Eli, a classics professor

47

in California, teaching and raising a family; his daughter, Eppy, a researcher on arctic wildlife, who took flying lessons, quit her day job, and hooked up as a pilot and part owner of a small fleet of puddle-jumpers that shuttles hunters, fishermen, and her old research buddies into the Alaskan wilds.

"Wow!" J'nelle says. "Now there's an independent woman for you!"

"Yeah. Proud of 'em both. They jumped way beyond me."

"Grandkids?"

"Bess and Sally," he says, "ten and eight. Eli's kids. They are ahead of me too—already fluent in two languages."

"Wow again."

"And you have a daughter."

"Yes," she says, "Anna. Adopted. I assume you can guess why."

He shoots her a questioning look.

"Abortions could be fairly crude back in those days," she says. "I was doing it without parental help."

He's heard the stories, even seen some of the gruesome pictures. He cannot imagine her parents—prominent, martini-drinking, country-clubber Christians—in the same frame with any of that.

"And where is she—Anna?"

"I don't know."

He gets out bowls and silverware, stirs the thickening broth, and looks at her. Her frame seems withdrawn, the shoulders slumped, the hair no longer bouncy but fallen from the dome of her skull. Her earrings hang without movement or sparkle.

He asks carefully: "Do you want to know?"

"Yes and no. It was an endless string of drug rehabs and relapses. The emotional strain wore me out, plus the hemorrhage of money to rehab centers and private detectives to trace her down, and the time I was spending on my own therapy and hers. The last time she vanished to God-knows-where, I made myself let it go."

"Where was Seth in all of this?"

"We adopted her in our late forties, and the worst of it was after he had vanished as well."

He hands her a bowl of stew, rimmed with the poking edges of clam shells.

"J'nelle, you've had a tough time of it."

She straightens and takes the bowl.

"I got tired of searching for vanished people. I got fed up with being vanished on. I got tired of crying alone in the dark. I just ... got tired, and I gave up."

In her eyes is that absent look that in the old days seemed to take her so far away and leave him so far behind. Now it is more the look of someone slammed against a wall.

She stands, holding the steaming bowl, and focuses her gaze on him.

"I'm afraid to know," she says. "I mean, my *own* daughter! I wake at night from screams I hear in my sleep. And I don't know whether they are my screams or hers or whether we are screaming at each other. I..."

She sets the bowl down and clasps the edge of the

counter. Her shoulders slump even more. She speaks as if talking to a face embedded in the countertop.

"Seth and I came to this island with her once when she was three years old. He was into surf fishing then, because he said it gave him peace. We stayed at an old hotel. I have no idea where on the island the hotel was, probably farther down the sound. Maybe that was another reason I wanted to come here this weekend, to chase another memory: Seth lost in his fishing; Anna with a blue and yellow plastic pail, running on her fat little legs through the surf, searching for shells. I suppose when you invited me down here, I thought maybe, if I got close to the place again, it would somehow bring those days back, revivify them. But I knew as soon as I turned onto the island it was not going to work. Rerunning old pictures through the mind is not enough."

She straightens, bows her head, and hugs her arms to her chest. Her shoulders begin to shake.

He sets down the stew he has ladled for himself. His hand, warm from holding the bowl, rests on the edge of the counter, fingers curled and folded. So many times in their years together she cried in just this way. Silent, shaken tears. They would be in his car, driving somewhere, or walking on a golf course late at night. A long pause would set in, like a drawn breath, and he would turn to see her in the posture he sees her in now, head lowered, face hidden, and it would take him a minute to see what was happening. And he froze each time, uncertain of what he should do because he was not sure what he himself would have wanted in that situation, or maybe because she brought him face-to-face with a human complexity that was so far beyond his imagining, he was afraid to try.

"Jesus," he says. "J'nelle, I'm sorry."

"And," she says, "the worst of it is—the part that makes me hurt the most—she may have had a child somewhere, a daughter, my one chance at being a grandparent, to start over and shower love on someone."

He picks up her bowl and his and sets them on the table, then turns and rests a hand on her shoulder.

"Have a seat," he says. "I'll open another bottle of wine. I suspect that before the evening is over, we may need it."

Friday Night

She helps carry the dirty dishes to the sink and, at his insistence, takes a seat in the sitting area of the room to answer emails while he finishes the cleaning up and loads the dishwasher. That done, he takes his glass of wine and the opened bottle and heads out to the porch and the stairs that lead to the upper deck.

"Come up when you've finished," he says, "but better put on a sweater or fleece or something. A cool evening is setting in."

Ten minutes later, she takes a seat next to him in another hammock chair he has turned to face the headlights cresting the inlet bridge. A black quilted jacket with gold embroidery is zipped to the soft depression at the base of her throat, and a memory pops into his brain of the ruddy blush that used to flood that depression when they made out. He would unbutton her blouse and watch as the blush spread to her chest. Now the depression is pale and shadowed by translucent tendons that seem strained to hang on.

"I sat here last night," he says, "watching those headlights come over the crest of the bridge and wondering what this visit would bring."

She takes a sip of wine and casts him a furtive glance before turning back to look at the sea.

"And?"

"I guess I'm still a bit confused," he says, "over why you came down here—to set things straight over you and Mason, rekindle old memories of Seth and Anna? I mean, it's great to see you, but, well, I'm just confused."

"I had not planned to tell you about Mason, and certainly not about the abortion. It's a constant source of grief and shame for me. But, I don't know, somewhere on the drive here from the airport, past those east Carolina swamps and fields that seem to stretch forever, it became clear to me that if I did not tell you, the weekend would feel false and very lonely."

"I know about the effect of those fields and swamps," he says. "They stir something in me, and I spend the rest of the drive trying to figure out what it is. In your case," he sighs, "it seems to have been a need to clear your conscience."

"That's a bit too succinct," she says.

He notices for the first time, consciously at least, the red taillights going in the opposite direction from the incoming headlights on the bridge. They are there, and then they vanish over the rim of the world.

"This conversation," he says, "feels very one-sided."

Her voice deepens like the evening light. "You remember that Valentine's Day cotillion I asked you to my senior year? You remember what happened?"

The claws of a shriveled memory scratch in a corner of his mind. "We had some sort of falling out. I wound up going with what's-her-name, Allison… something."

"Allison Winslett."

"Yeah. You're not still upset about that, are you?"

"I thought you understood how much that cotillion meant to me, that it was a chance for me to prove something I'd wanted to prove for so long to everyone at that dance, and to myself. I wasn't pretty or part of the in-crowd, and I had worked so hard to make up for that, to be a good student, athlete, and student leader. That cotillion was a chance for me to prove there was something more to me than Miss Know-It-All and Miss Do-It-All."

"You *were* something other than a Miss Know-It-All. People liked you; they elected you class president."

"No. I wanted them to see the 'me' beneath all that. I wanted them to see us on the dance floor, whispering, snuggling, holding hands—that special thing we had that most of them just dreamed about—and know I was a person with deep feelings who could fall in love and glow with it. I wasn't pretty or popular, but I had that. I had you; I had us. And then you bailed and those hopes came crashing down. My parents had to scramble to get me a date. Bobby Ravenel came all the way from Montgomery."

Around him, the night's silence stirs and hums and grows louder. In the cup of his hands, the half-full bowl of the wine glass feels huge and empty. He starts to speak but catches himself. Yes, he knew about all of that, about what it meant to her. He knew from clues he had picked up that, for all her achievements—class president, straight-A student, swimming team, tennis

54

team—she felt out of it socially. She thought those sharp, angular features and quick eyes—so attractive to him now as well as then—didn't compare to the soft, round faces of the beauty queens featured in the Oneonta High yearbook, floating in the flounce of their hooped evening gowns. And he knew that somehow being with him helped her make up for that. He knew all of that, yet he stood her up. Why?

"I know," she says, "it was just a teenage dream, but it was so strong. It seemed so meant to be. And then it wasn't."

He stares out at the gathering darkness. No moon or stars yet, but there is that sense of clouds somewhere out of sight, moving in to steal the night.

"I needed that dream, Ace," she says, "at that time in my life. I wanted to be there with you."

"Yes," he says. "I wanted to be there with you too."

"Then why?"

The wine glass feels even larger now, as if he is holding a globe. The plaited ropes of his hammock chair press into the bend of his spine.

"I don't know," he says. "Maybe I was jealous, resentful of your accomplishments. Maybe I saw you slipping away. Or maybe I was just adolescent, selfish, and stupid."

He draws in a deep breath and lets it out slowly. If he tried to rise, it would be like heaving himself from a dark hole.

"Or maybe in some unconscious way, I sensed your fling with Mason Morrel."

"It wasn't a fling."

"OK, sorry."

"And Mason wasn't even on the scene then, at least not as far as I was concerned."

He heaves a frustrated sigh. "I shouldn't have called it that. It's just that, I didn't mean … Shit, I don't know what I mean."

Silence hovers between them, darting its eyes. It is as if they have both settled into their spaces on the deck and become part of the dim evening. When she speaks, her voice seems to come from far away.

"After Bobby Ravenel brought me home from the party, I lay in bed in the mushy smell of tears and teenage grief and felt truly alone for the first time since I met you. The bed seemed very small, the room detached and afloat as if I was drifting away from that party and all the silly hopes and fantasies I'd left there. I felt foolish and stupid, and I hated that."

"Yes, I know the feeling."

"Well, it was there in that dark bedroom that I began to flee the life I had tried so hard to create for myself. For the first time since we started dating, I allowed my thoughts to venture beyond you and me and high school to what might lie ahead."

He sees himself, back there on that dance floor, peeking over Allison Winslett's freckled shoulder for glimpses of J'nelle, that selfish, idiot boy, weighted with the dread of someone who has stumbled—no, pushed himself—through an unseen barrier into a strange and uncharted land.

"What I remember about that dance," he says, "is watching you with some guy I didn't know and feeling even more of whatever it was that made me bail on you in the first place. And I also remember now, having thought about it, that Mason was there, and he was sort of hanging around you, trying to be close."

So when did it begin, Ace thinks, there at the Valentine's Day dance or later when he saw them talking at the end of the hallway or somewhere in between?

"He made it clear he was interested," she says, "back in the fall when I first walked into his class. It was as if he was extending his hand to help me make the leap from where I was."

"Hello, scholars!" Mason would say when the class was seated. "What a bright-eyed, brainy bunch! Ready to rumble? Let's talk about dreams, where they come from, what they tell us, how they lead to stories. Who has a dream they're willing to share to help us get started?"

And he, Ace, had volunteered—some adolescent dream about his girlfriend who had gone off to college. What a sap!

"And," J'nelle adds, breaking into Ace's thoughts, "he seemed to care, to really care."

"So," Ace says, "what became of old Mason?"

"When I told him I was pregnant, he fled the scene, sent money for the abortion—no card or letter with it, just bills in an envelope. I think, after your senior year, he and his wife moved to Texas. That's the last I heard of him."

Texas had always seemed another country to Ace. So

big. A place to get lost.

"I blew it, J'nelle," he says. "I'm sorry. I was just, well like I said, stupid."

"And perhaps a little heartless—at least it felt that way to me."

"Yes," he says, "I guess so."

"But handsome," she says. "Allison seemed pleased with herself."

"I have no idea."

He can't remember what the fight that precipitated the whole mess was about. Almost certainly, she will know, but to ask would be one more sign of his callousness. Besides, he *does* know what it was about—the real reason. Resentment, jealousy, fear of losing her. What if he had been more of a man? What if that dance had happened the way she dreamed? How would that have changed their lives?

From beneath them comes the sound of clawed feet on the front porch.

She grabs the arm of his chair. "What is that?"

"Raccoon. Pays a visit every night." He glances at his watch. "Tonight he's ahead of schedule."

The scratching continues in a meandering pattern across the porch, pausing, then moving on.

She relaxes back into her chair.

"A dark messenger," she says.

"More like a thief searching for food."

"Even thieves bring messages."

The scratching sounds fade toward the far edge of the porch, then stop.

"Definitely a messenger," she says. "I watch for messengers these days."

"For news of what?"

"I'm not quite sure, but I feel an urgency to know where my life is headed. I've left so much behind, or it's left me. I feel adrift. Seth is gone, Anna. My work is sporadic. I feel a need to know."

"Don't we all," he says, "but we can't know the future."

"No, but you can try to understand how you got to where you are. And so lately my mind has been turning toward the past, searching for clues. How did I get to this place that feels so like a precipice? Those things that happened in high school, college, and through the years, how did they shape my life, and did they even happen as I remember them? Did I miss something? Did I add something? I want to find the true story of my life instead of just continuing to muddle through it."

"You haven't muddled through it."

"You don't know the whole story."

Now he feels on a precipice. They are both there, two people looking down, not quite daring to hold hands.

"You can't know the past any more than you can know the future," he says.

"Maybe," she says, "but you can try to see things more clearly, figure out how they fit in to everything else, understand better what they mean."

He emits a slight chuckle.

"You don't buy it," she says.

"When I revisit my past," he says, "I catch myself

lying, and before I know it, I've lost the truth entirely, if it was ever really there to find in the first place."

"Yes," she says, "that's how it seems to work, and that's why I want to go back and peel away the self-deception. I want to know the truth. It's become a compulsion."

He is about to say, *Darlin', where you are concerned, that ain't nothin' new*, when she says:

"And I realized about a year ago that it begins with what happened between us in high school. And that's why I got in touch with you again, or at least one of the reasons. There's the real answer to your question about why I'm here."

He sips the last drops of wine from his glass. They always taste thinner and less sweet than the ones before.

"Do you understand what I'm saying?" she says.

He rests his head back against the top of the chair. The breeze tickles his hair. The night itself seems nervous.

"I'm not sure."

"I guess it's more accurate to say: what I'm *asking*?"

"It might help to hear you say it."

"Before we got to know each other, I had a real crisis of confidence." She pauses. "You remember my parents?"

"Yes, they never seemed happy with me."

"They weren't happy with anything. They were alcoholic, emotional dead zones, spouting lofty plans for me without a clue who I was. I was their vehicle for fulfilling their own lost dreams, and they put on a lot of pressure. I was terrified of failure and afraid of living a future that wasn't mine. And then you came along, and there was someone who liked me in spite of my self-doubt and who wanted to hold me and kiss me, and he was as lost as I was."

"I was lost?"

"Yes, and that was important, because when we were together, when we got close, my fear melted away. I wasn't alone. I felt warm and safe."

She takes an ample swig of wine, presses her thighs together, and lowers the glass to rest on them, cupping it in her hands in a reverential way.

"That saved me," she said, "from anorexia or bulimia or something even worse. I was on a slow walk toward the edge of a cliff."

"Another precipice," he says.

"Exactly."

"I didn't see any of that back then," he says. "It seemed to me you pretty much had it together all along, and then for a while we did, and then it was gone."

Another moment of silence.

"Maybe," she says, "if you go along with what I'm asking, we can figure all that out. So I guess the question is: would you like to do it together?"

"Do what, exactly?"

"Search for the truth. About us, about each other, about ourselves."

He feels a reflexive instinct to duck, as if a spear has been launched at him from his past. Somewhere out there in the night, the raccoon is at work, bent to its grubby task, scratching its fingers into the drippy black muck of the marsh for a clam. Cloud-filtered moonlight falling on its head and back. Mask across its eyes that see so well, so very well, in the dark.

She holds out her wine glass. "I could use a replenishment. Saying all of that wasn't easy."

He pours wine in her glass, then his. His hand trembles. The bottle neck taps against the rims of the glasses.

"Have I made you nervous?"

"No, I'm OK."

"I don't mean to drag you into something you don't want to do."

"It's OK," he says.

A moment of silence passes before she says, "Should I ask my question again or just drop the whole thing and enjoy the weekend?"

It dawns on him that from the moment he invited her to the beach, he has had no plan for what they would do other than meals and laughs and reminiscences over fuzzy memories of the past. No plan for where it might lead. And then she came, this new, older J'nelle, dragging her past with her, trying to drag their past—their real past, whatever in the hell it was—the Mason thing, the abortion, the guilt trip over the cotillion—right out into the open. He tries to recall the images from those old times, of them together, that were so vivid to him not more than twenty-four hours ago as he sat alone on this very deck, but all he gets is a kaleidoscope of silhouettes.

"I've thought about trying to go back there and somehow relive those times," he says. "Verify that what happened was real. But it wasn't, was it? It was what you just said it was: a teenage dream, puppy love, whatever they call it, very real at the time, good while it lasted, then poof! Gone."

She rests back in her chair. A breeze has picked up with the nightfall. He imagines it flowing over the contours of her face, brushing her hair from her temples.

"No, Ace," she says, "there has to have been more to it than that, because remnants of those feelings are still there."

When he does not respond, she takes a generous sip of wine.

"Still *here*, I mean," she says.

"Are they?"

Once again she bends into that prayerful posture, holding her wine glass like a chalice.

"Don't you want to know?"

He leans forward with his arms on his knees, wine glass cupped in his hands in a copy of her.

"Maybe, I guess."

She cants her head to look at him. "Does that mean you're willing to join me in the great quest?"

"Not willing, but I will."

"Thanks," she says. "It means so much."

"I have a feeling," he says, "this will not be easy."

"No," she says, "probably not."

The wine bottle is almost empty. He offers her the last drops.

She places a hand over the top of her glass.

"No thanks," she says, "I'm over my limit," then finishes off her last swallow. "It's been a long day. I think I'll go to bed, read my usual two-and-a-half pages of my current novel, and fall asleep."

"OK," he says, "I'll see you in the morning."

She rises to leave and starts toward the stairs leading down to the front porch.

"There should be some towels in the closet in your bathroom," he says.

She pauses at the top of the stairs, then turns and comes back to bend and give him a soft peck on the cheek, her lips cool and wet from the wine.

"We'll be OK, Ace." she says. "We can do this, and help each other understand it all, and we'll be just fine."

Then she is gone. Her steps echo down the stairs to the porch, then across the main room's floor on the way to her bedroom.

He throws back the remains of his wine, rests forward again with his elbows on his knees, and stares out at the night. Below where he sits, toward the rear of the house, her bedroom light comes on and casts a glow upon the leaves of an ancient live oak that all but covers the driveway. She is there now, in that room, moving about, changing for bed, maybe preparing to take a shower. On his cheek, the last trace of her goodnight peck lingers like a summons, gently delivered to suck away any anger left from the news about her and Mason Morrel. He should have been prepared for this. He should have had a plan. He should have known from his dreams alone what could happen.

Pam's silent warning: *You could get hurt*.

And he was hurt, not more than an hour into her visit, a hurt that feels strangely like a slaughter, by this woman below him in the lit bedroom, J'nelle the stranger, the summoner, now on to her next task, her end-of-the-day routines: the tending of skin, hair, and nails, selection of clothing for tomorrow—those women things he saw Pam do for fifty years that are to him still mysterious.

And they will always be so, he thinks, *and after all this time, who cares?*

But back there in those high school days, he cared in a visceral way. He imagined what the young J'nelle was doing in those late night hours before bed, what intimate secrets got performed in the inner-sanctum of her bedroom, steeped in the smells of powder and perfume and all those other things girls used. The warm-honey smell of her washed hair; the fresh, clean smell of her ironed clothes carefully folded in her bureau that was, as he pictured it, lacquered white or cream with spooled legs and thin rings of gold between the spools. Maybe there were banners on the wall, stuffed animals propped against her pillows. Maybe there was a small desk, also lacquered white, with a crook-necked lamp where she did her homework. He imagined the imprint of her slender feet in the deep pile rug, the quick movement of her calves and ankles as she got into bed. All there, so vividly he could almost touch it. And he never got so much as a glimpse.

He never had—he could never have had—the nerve to try.

The branches of the live oak go dark. The great gray owl that calls almost nightly from the grove east of the house is silent. Out beyond the dunes, the relentless surf washes in and out, stealing sand from the shore, moving slowly in his direction.

He pulls out his cell phone, checks the Series score—Final: Sox 6, Dodgers 2. At least that's going right, but Fenway Park in Boston, where they are playing, seems so far away. And the storm, maybe he should check it as well. He clicks on the weather app, but gets only the spinning circle of a slow-loading connection.

"Fuck it," he says and heads to bed.

Saturday morning

He cooks eggs and bacon and mulls over last night's conversation, like a lawyer reconstructing a case. What exactly did he commit to? What led him to do it? And how did all of that talk and reminiscing lead to those fantasies he had later of the young J'nelle in her bedroom with its shadows and smells, doing those things girls do to get ready for bed? It all flowed so seamlessly, but now it does not seem seamless. It seems scattered and twisted, stretched between different realities.

The older J'nelle is no doubt performing an early morning version of that bedroom routine right now, the things women do to stop age in its tracks and revive suggestions of youth. It's tough, he knows, watching it go. There's a horror in it, like the horror he felt yesterday when he caught a glimpse of himself in the bathroom mirror. Does she have those feelings? She didn't like her looks in high school, but by any measure she was attractive, and she had a lot more to lose in that category than he did. So, perhaps it's more brutal for her, watching herself shrink and evaporate at the same time.

Maybe that's it. Maybe the "in search of my true past" routine she laid on him last night is just another gambit to escape the great evaporation.

Her deck sneakers squeak on the floor as she enters the room from the hallway. Whatever she has done in the makeup shop of her bathroom has worked. The beauty she brought with her yesterday is back in a bright-new-morning kind of way and chases away the shadows lingering from their evening's talk. He pours a mug of coffee and holds it out to her. She accepts it, rests her backside against the counter, and takes a first sip.

"Good morning," she says in a burry, slightly bemused voice.

She's wearing jeans and a chartreuse top under a loose cotton flannel shirt, a step down from yesterday's dressier linen. Or maybe a step up, depending. Or maybe just, well, neither. He needs to relax, not overreact to the startling radiance she has brought into this usually very empty room.

"G' morning," he says as he pops a couple of slices of bread into the toaster oven.

"There are ghosts here," she says. "I can feel them. I guess you know that."

"Yes. Sinclairs too stubborn to leave. Not untypical, but harmless."

"How about the hurricane?"

"I checked on it. Not harmless, Category 2, headed north-northeast, which would be roughly where we are standing. Could be throwing rain our way by late tomorrow."

"What about landfall?"

"Few days at the earliest. Nothing to worry about; you'll be on the road home by then."

"Probably you should be too."

"Maybe. I'll keep an eye on it."

"What do you do about the house?"

"Shut it up. Those old pine shutters on the windows have worked for a long time. Once a fallen tree damaged the roof. I've cut some of them back since then."

She pushes herself off the counter next to him and moves around to the other side of the island to face his back as he works at the stove.

"So when did you become such a risk-taker," she says. "I never saw you that way, then I heard you joined the marines and went to Vietnam."

"Not quite the way it happened. I was about to be drafted, so I joined the army, went to OCS, and my artillery unit got assigned to the marines."

"How did that work out?"

He gets these questions from time to time, at gatherings—cocktail parties, family reunions—from people who have no clue. "I was lucky," he always says, "I'm still here," and thinks, *How the fuck do you think it worked out?*

"'Fun, fun, fun,'" he says to J'nelle, "'till our daddy takes our T-bird away.'"

"Where were you?"

"I Corps, near the DMZ."

"When?"

"'68 and '69."

"That was the big Tet Offensive, right?"

"Right."

"Seth was there," she says, "twice—then and later."

"Marine?"

"Yes, infantry."

"Jesus, he probably had even more fun than I did."

"And what kind of fun did you have?"

Ace's fingers tighten on the spatula.

"I got hit in the leg and chest by shrapnel from a Russian-made rocket."

"Seriously?"

"I can show you the scars."

He lets go of the spatula, grabs the cooking fork, and jabs at the frying bacon, flipping it about.

"I'm open to hearing about it," she says, "if you feel like telling me."

He has never spoken about it before, except to Pam and a VA shrink who was trying to treat him for PTSD.

"It was the night before Christmas, and all through the house ... well, not exactly. But it was Christmas Eve, and the cooks had brought a chocolate cake to the bunker where I was fire direction officer. I sat down on a foot locker, where we stored our maps and slide rules, and raised my cooking mess fork to dig into a big slab of that cake when I heard an ear-splitting bang right overhead and felt something big and hot tear into my chest. It was like being hit with an axe. I was off the foot locker, on my back on the dirt floor, deaf from the sound, and there was dust everywhere from where the rocket had shredded the sandbags on top of the bunker, and my first thought was that the bastards had ruined my cake, the only piece of chocolate cake I'd seen since we left the States. My legs were jerking. My arms were twitching.

The wounds in my chest and leg felt like they were on fire. And then I kind of woke up and thought, *I'm going to die, right here in this godforsaken bunker in the middle of this surreal life created for me by the dark forces of my own country.* And then I thought, *No, worse: I'm going to be paralyzed*, 'cause a marine officer I'd made friends with had had his spine severed in an ambush a few days before. I tried to get up to see how bad others in the bunker were hurt but couldn't make myself move. People were shouting from outside, and I heard another rocket scream in and hit nearby, and then another, and someone ripped my blouse open and pressed a bandage to my chest, and the medic jammed the needle in, and the next thing I know, I'm being off-loaded from a chopper onto this hospital ship called *The Sanctuary*, and this Navy surgeon is standing over me telling me to hang on and he'll have me screwing every nurse on the ship in less than two weeks. And then everything went blank, and I came to after surgery, and over the course of the next year, I found out the two weeks was bullshit and so was the nurse part, and there began a life-long distrust of doctors that carried over into my legal career. And so, that's the size of it: bang, hurt, down, restored, but no nurses and no chocolate cake."

He takes a deep breath. The toaster oven emits a sharp ding.

"Everybody in the bunker was killed except the cook who brought the cake and me."

He turns his head slightly to speak over his shoulder in her direction. "Does that take care of it?"

"Sorry," she says in a slightly tremulous tone.

"Why?"

"For what happened, for asking."

"It's OK," he says.

She blows steam off her coffee and takes a long, slow sip. "Ace…"

"Yes?"

"Are you sure you're restored?"

That tremor in his hand and wrist again. He tightens his grip on the fork, suspended and dripping over the frying bacon.

"What makes you ask that?"

"It matters to me."

He turns from the stove and looks at her. She takes another sip of coffee and looks back.

"Really," she says, "it does."

Against the dark oak beams in the ceiling at the far end of the room, the sandy sparkles in her hair look brighter than the day before, almost mesmerizing. A new set of earrings, discs of aqua stone rimmed in gold, remind him of the ocean two days ago before the clouds moved in—deep limitless blue under a peekaboo sun. Her look comes at him straight out of their conversation of the night before.

He turns back to the stove.

"I don't know," he says. "Hard to tell about those things."

"Seth was wounded too, but he was shot in the chest."

"How the hell did he survive that?"

"Same way you did, I guess. They took him to that

same ship, *The Sanctuary*. He wouldn't talk about it—any of it. It was like a darkness settled over those war years of his life and from there a shadow spread slowly over the rest of it. He was never restored."

"You think that's what his disappearance was all about?"

"Yes. The physical disappearance and the mental and emotional one that began long before that. By the end, he was a ghost on a Harley motorcycle."

She pauses. "And a drugged-up, drunken ghost at home."

He forks out the bacon onto a paper towel, drains grease from the skillet, and pours in the blended eggs. While they are cooking, a quick spread of butter on the toast. Fat, cholesterol… ta-da, ta-da. Pearlman would have a fit, devout medicine man that he is, but he doesn't approve of wine and Scotch either. The eggs hiss and bubble on the hot iron, and Ace has a flash memory of a picture he saw of Seth at one of the earlier Oneonta High reunions he did not attend, a thin, gaunt-looking guy, with a rock-hard chest and wrists and forearms that looked like they could deliver a handshake that would clamp your whole body. But at the fiftieth reunion, Seth had changed into someone almost unrecognizable, puffy face and cheeks that seemed to squeeze shut his eyes, a body straight off the beer and hot dog line at a football game.

"I'm sorry it turned out that way," he says, "for you both."

"It was killing me too," she says. "If he hadn't

disappeared, I would have found a way to disappear myself, at least from him."

"And you still don't know what happened?"

Her cup scrapes in slow rhythm as she swishes it back and forth over the countertop.

"I know what happened," she says. "About a year ago, I was going through some of his things: boxes of papers, magazines, and books. He was keeping a journal—not a diary, more a stream-of-consciousness narrative full of his own writing and excerpts from magazines and newspapers, poems he liked, stories. It filled several boxes and his writings raved at times, but also dazzled, the way his mind jumped from one thing to another and yet somehow brought it all together—not logically but on an emotional level like poetry.

"Anyway, the last forty or so pages of it were about glaciers, particularly the Diamond Peak Glacier in southwest Alaska. It was breaking up. Giant crevasses were forming, and one of them was estimated to go down at least two hundred feet. There were photos looking into it: sunlit, translucent jade at the top, then deepening into blue-green, then into a blue so blue and deep it seemed part of another world, then into blackness, absolute nothing. And in this part of the journal, Seth made no entries of his own. The dancing prose that connected the rest of it went silent. It was as if he'd arrived somewhere, and there was no more to say."

The cup stops scraping the countertop. Her eyes focus on it as if she has found a centerpoint.

"So," he says, "you think he went to see that glacier and the crevasse and fell in."

"No," she says, "he didn't fall. He jumped. It's perfect: that hard-ass marine thing that followed him out of the war would sooner or later demand he do something to escape the confusion and pain—not just end it all by shooting himself or taking pills, but escape it, make the leap into whatever, even if it was a dark, icy oblivion."

"Jesus," Ace says.

Her lips are tightly set with tiny creases at the corners, her eyes flashing and adamant.

"Did they search the glacier?" he asks.

"No. And if they had they wouldn't have found anything. I know Seth; when he leaped into oblivion he would have been sure not to leave a trace."

Ace feels another tremor coming on and tightens his grip on the spatula handle. But it is not a tremor this time; it comes from somewhere else. An image of himself frozen in place on the vast plain of that glacier, desperate to reach out and grasp the shirttail of a ghost—Seth's, his own, the ghost of some other nameless, faceless vet—to keep it from going over the edge into that deep blue night.

"How do you deal with that?" he says. He means it as a general question—how does *anyone* deal with something like that?—but it comes out sounding as a demand to know.

"I was so tired of it by then, so utterly worn out with his shit and Anna's, that I let myself label what he did as pure selfishness so I could dodge yet another round of guilt and what ifs—if I had only done this or that, seen how bad it was, nagged him into therapy one more time."

"How did that work out—the dodge?"

"How do you think it worked out?"

Touché, he thinks.

He scrapes the eggs onto two plates, adds the bacon and toast, and holds her plate out to her. She is resting with her elbows on the counter, staring down at her coffee cup as if reading the dregs. He sets her plate on the counter before her.

"Let's eat."

He pours them more coffee. They take their seats at the old walnut dining table like awkward birds settling into a lakeside nest. She taps a finger on his wrist before he can pick up his fork.

"When I asked you to join me on a journey into our pasts last night, I didn't intend for us to dive right into the darkness."

"Yeah, I assumed it would be only about the happy, carefree days of youth—parties, rock-and-roll, and teenage sex." He clears his throat. "Or the lack thereof."

She gives him a teasing smile. "Maybe we can visit those memories later, or, as you say, the lack thereof."

She nibbles at her toast, takes up her fork and begins to pick at her eggs.

"But now that we're there, in the darkness, I need to say a bit more about my part in it."

"More stuff like Mason."

76

"No, larger than that."

"The abortion."

"After the abortion," she says. "What happened next."

"Is this another confession?"

"It's just something I need to say."

Ah, yes—that must-do personality, the straight-A student who did all her homework every night and hugged it to her chest when she walked in the door to school. He was not a do-all-your-homework-every-night kind of guy.

"And why do you need me to hear it?"

"It's about you, indirectly, and about Seth, because of your roles in the military. I never had the nerve to tell him about it. But during our talk last night, I felt some of that warmth from the old days seep back. I feel safe."

She takes a squirrel-sized nip of toast and continues to pick at her eggs with her dangling fork. *For God's sake*, he thinks, *eat something!*

"During my last year of college and the early days of grad school, when you and he were in Vietnam, I was heavy into the protest movement."

"If I hadn't been otherwise engaged, I probably would have been too."

"No. I mean really heavy—screaming obscenities at cops and guardsmen, sitting in at public buildings, pouring blood on the steps of induction centers, getting arrested, calling people like you and Seth child murderers. For about two weeks, I was in SDS until I found out that the group I was with cared more about sex and drugs than saving the world from American imperialism. But I was such a believer, so chock full of moral certainty."

"You were young."

"I was an arrogant shit, another version of that intellectual arrogance I affected in high school. It was a cover."

"For what?"

She drops her fork and stares at her plate. "Insecurity, uncertainty, fear of something, sort of like that fear I told you about in high school before I met you."

She raises her eyes to his. They seem imploring, hesitant.

"Does what I've just told you about my role in the protests piss you off?"

"No," he says. "Does what I just told you about Vietnam scare you away?"

The question pops in his brain: *scare her away from what?*

"No," she says, "it doesn't."

She braces her elbows on the edge of the table, rests her chin on her fists.

"I'd heard you were over there, and the more I got into the counterculture protest stuff, the more you began to haunt me, like the Ghost of Christmas Past that used to scare me as a kid. You'd come near dawn, which was about the time I went to bed. It seemed weird. I thought I'd left us behind."

"I've never been a ghost before. What did I look like?"

"You didn't look like anything. You were just there."

"You sure it was me? Maybe it was guilt."

"I thought you said yesterday that I wasn't into guilt."

"It could be that maybe, perhaps, just possibly, I was wrong."

She forks a quick bite of eggs. "You're right; that's exactly what it was.

"By then I'd seen a doctor, and I knew what the abortion had done: I'd killed not only the fetus but my youth and my secret, tender hopes for the future. It seemed like a punishment. And maybe it was the look in your eyes in that haunting, a look of complete, unknowing blankness, that showed me that the road that led me to where I was ran all the way back to that night in high school, after the botched cotillion, when I lay in bed and decided with such conviction to break free of my old life and rush off into, where? I had not a clue. But off I went, and this is where it had led: a woman who had destroyed her most cherished dreams and was now staying up all night, screaming at cops, taking LSD, and pouring blood."

She lays down her fork and stares at the table beyond the edge of her plate, then once again raises her eyes to stare into his. In high school, her temples seemed translucent and vulnerable, veins running like tiny rivers just out of sight. Now the veins braid their way beneath the weathered landscape of her face.

He says, "Is this the point where I'm supposed to say, 'You're too hard on yourself'?"

"You *are* pissed off."

"No. Well, yeah maybe. But not so much at you. Back then the war, drugs, protests, the whole scene was a mess."

"When all is said and done," she says, "I think that's why I married Seth, as some muddle-headed effort at redemption."

"For what?"

"My excesses. That thing in me that caused me to commit them: abortion, SDS, drugs, running off with Mason. Leaving you."

"How did Seth redeem that?"

"He showed up at UVA, fresh out of the marines, the spring semester of my second year in grad school. He'd left after his sophomore year. I was sitting with a friend on the front steps of The Rotunda when I saw him get off the bus at the stop on Rugby Road. He had on a marine tee shirt and combat fatigues tucked into worn-out combat boots, and he stepped off that bus and started across Main Street toward the Alderman Library as if he had just stepped out of that war I'd been so worked up over and knew nothing about, including the people in it. You could see it in the way he walked, more of a slog than a walk, and the way he moved—something cautious and alert about it. He seemed starved in some way that was more than physical. His body was small, hardened, and tense, and he looked so alive, and so conscious of being alive. I couldn't take my eyes off him. He was different from all the people around me. He was real."

In her voice is a hint of excitement, not heard since she first stepped into the house.

"And so...," he says.

"So I latched on to him, I mean right there. I walked up to him and said something goofy like, 'Welcome to campus; I haven't seen you before.' And I walked him over to the engineering school where he was already a week late to register, and then we met later for coffee. He didn't say much, but that attracted me to him even more, because all I'd heard for the past two years was people arguing, talking over each other, and shouting. And so we tried another way of communicating, which was being as close as we could get physically, lying next to each other and hugging, and almost endless sex, and that seemed to ease the guilt I felt over my protest behavior except for those nights when he would thrash about and shout in his sleep and I would lie awake and stare into the darkness and realize it was nothing like the darkness he was in. I'd never seen terror before. He'd shout and thrash until the only way to make the terror go away was to wake him up and have more sex. It was kind of like a drug for us, a quick fix that was sure not to last."

"What was the phrase?—'whatever turns you on.' At least it worked for a while."

"I look back on all of that now and realize that while I thought I was helping him, what I was really doing was getting out of my own head."

"The universal condition of youth," he says. "In high school, I used to look in the mirror, and the last person I wanted to see was staring back at me, the person I was trying so hard not to be. I kind of panicked and all sorts of shit started to happen."

"Like Allison Winslett and the cotillion debacle."

"Probably—and a bunch of other stuff, like a couple of nights in a Pickens County jail for liberating ten cases of beer from a Miller High Life truck."

"When did that happen?"

"My senior year, after you quit writing me. Also, dynamiting an old man's pile of cans he'd collected from beside the road, because he'd taken a shot at Bobby, Ellis, and me; and lighting a string of cherry bombs and throwing it under Mrs. Patton's desk in the library the last day of school. You remember her, the Battle-Axe of the Books. That one almost closed the show. They weren't going to let me graduate."

"That's how you 'got out of yourself'?"

"I wasn't very good at it."

"Neither was I."

She looks down at her cold eggs, takes a sip of coffee, then lowers the cup and hangs her head.

"The truth is, I ache over Seth. He was a good man, and before the war, he was a good boy, and that boy was still there hanging on when we were together. I didn't see it, or I didn't know what to do with it, except to give him more sex. He kept a three-by-five American flag pinned to the wall above our bed. His high school track trophies were perched on our bureau and bookshelf, all around the room. On the floor next to the bed was his old Hopalong Cassidy throw rug. I didn't have a clue.

It's just another example of Miss Know-It-All screwing up. I thought because I made A's in high school and college, I could handle anything in spite of all the evidence I had accumulated to the contrary. And before it was over, of course, I'd just made it worse."

She shakes her head slowly back and forth. The ends of her hair brush along her jaw and the back of her neck.

"Seth needed a deep, special kind of love," she says. "He wanted open displays of affection, terms of endearment: sweetie, sugar, darling. Impromptu hugs and kisses. I gave him sex and indulged my usual compulsion to try to fix everything and make it right."

"Well, you tried," he says, "and I'm guessing the sex wasn't all that bad."

Her head stops shaking, but remains bowed, her eyes still staring at her plate.

He rests a finger on her arm.

"J'nelle, it was a crazy time. We all screwed up. The world was screwed up. And the best way to go with it now is to try and forget it."

She wipes away a tear and looks at him.

"I don't believe that. I think we have to fight and at least try to keep those horrors from happening again."

He rises quickly from the table, tosses his plate and silverware in the sink with a clatter, and turns on the tap.

"Oh really—and what the hell would that mean exactly for people like us, here in our peachy, beachy, comfy upper-middle-class lives? We claim lofty ideals, but

83

we're too comfortable or lazy to fight for them. Just like our counterparts in the '50s and '60s who let a bunch of ignorant bastards lead us into a useless war…"

He shuts off the tap turns to face her.

"…that killed and maimed a shitload of people. One thing about you has not changed: you still want to make it all right, everything—past, present, and future. And, you know, that's really not possible. So, why don't you just give it the fuck up?"

He turns back to the sink, runs hot water to make suds, and begins to scour the skillet and cooking fork. He hears her chair scrape, and then she is beside him at the sink. She lets her plate and silverware slide into the water, then takes his arm, pulls him away from the sink, and encircles her arms about his waist, pressing him close, resting her wet cheek against his shoulder. Her hair is full of that honey-warm smell he remembers from past times, a mysterious confection of young girl's air-dried locks and shampoo.

He starts to mumble something, but it is cut off by a tremor that sends the cooking fork he is still holding into a rat-a-tat-tat against the sink.

She raises her face to him, a look he has not seen in a long time, of soft, soulful interest. He used to see it when they were close, say after a hug when she stepped back to study him in a way that hung a giant, invisible question mark.

He glances down at the fork and stops the shake by pressing it against the stainless-steel sink.

"Getting old is not worth a shit," he says.

"I know," she says, "it sucks. But so far we've survived, and I'm so glad."

THEY DRIVE DOWN the island to a stretch of beach away from the crowds, park in a space tucked in among the dunes, and walk along the sand. Fishermen have driven four-wheelers and pickups onto the strand and sit in folding chairs drinking beer, or stand in waders and fish the surf. The day is cool. The sky hangs above them in strings of octopus gray. An offshore wind whips the heavy air in thick gusts. Waves heave themselves against eroding cliffs of sand that break and slosh into the water.

"See, doomed," he says. "Nature is coming for us."

"Don't think about that now," she says. "Let's just *be* for a change."

He identifies the shorebirds for her, the same ones they saw yesterday: willets, plovers, oystercatchers, sanderlings, and a new species, a curlew, plodding on its skinny legs, holding at the ready its long, curved bill, as it searches the washed-over, bubbling sand.

"He seems pickier than the others," she says.

"Very patient and careful," he says. "I could learn a thing or two."

Once they are past the fishermen, the beach is deserted. The thud and hiss of waves and the calls of circling gulls fill the silence between them. They find a sea-sculpted driftwood log to sit on and watch the surf.

"What is it about the ocean," she says, "that soothes and heals?"

"It speaks from the realm of the deep unconscious."

"Wow. Quick answer."

"It's from Jung," he says. "I studied him in the agony of one of my mid-life crises. A lot of it rings with new age bullshit, but I think there's something to it."

"You've had mid-life crises?"

"Some would say I'm still in one."

"I sort of picked that up between the lines of your emails," she says.

"What did I say that told you that?"

"I guess it takes one to know one."

"I would not have imagined that about you before today—that you are someone who might have mid-life crises. You always seemed so together. Even at the reunions, you seemed like the line from Bob Dylan's song, 'forever young.'"

"I love that song, but it's a dream, and sometimes a fairly cruel one."

"Yes, it is."

They sit for another half-hour then start back toward the car. When they reach the wet sand near the water, their hands come together and lock in a light touch of crooked fingers. His throat clogs with lumpy questions. At the higher stretch of beach, chunks of sand continue to break off into the water. "Thump!" go the waves, then leave seconds of silence before the next one hits. A line comes to him from James Joyce's *A Portrait of the Artist as a Young Man*: "Am I walking into eternity along Sandymount Strand?"

"I am not ready for that," he whispers to himself,

and then realizes that, as he often does when he's alone, he has said it out loud.

She lets her hand slip away.

"No, not your hand," he says. "I didn't mean that."

"What, then?"

"I guess where my life is heading."

"To that 'undiscovered country,'" she says, "'from whose bourn no traveler returns.'"

He stops and looks at her. His hand feels suddenly empty.

"Thank you, Prince Hamlet," he says. "I didn't know you were a Shakespeare scholar."

"We read it in high school," she says. "Remember? Lately that line has been popping up."

Ah, yes—that unerring, near-photographic memory.

"Thanks," he says, "for reminding me. Always a welcome thought."

Back at the car, she wonders out loud about the hurricane, and when they are on the road and pick up a cell signal, he gives her his phone and shows her the weather app. She checks on the forecast as they drive.

"Still Category 2," she says, "still headed toward the coast, may increase to Category 3 or higher, may not; may reverse course and hit Cuba, may not; may veer out to sea, may hit the eastern seaboard. In other words, they don't have a clue."

"Probably the latter option," he says, "about where we are now—just a hunch."

"When did you become such a pessimist?" she says.

"Pam used to ask that question."

"And?"

"Somewhere along the way," he says. "Maybe when the shell hit that bunker, or maybe when what we had in high school fell apart, or maybe even before that." He pauses. "But you're not a pessimist."

"No," she says, "I just move on."

"Yes," he says, "indeed you do," and says to himself, *from just about everything.*

Saturday, midday

He drives them down the island to a small restaurant called The Whale Head, where they find a table next to a large window that looks out over a boat dock in the sound. The boats rock and yank their dock lines. Halyards clack in the wind.

The waitress is a stout, middle-aged Black woman with a pixie haircut. Her hands and wrists move with quick certainty. The soft features of her face seem permanently fixed in a smile, but there is a hint of watchful concern in the way her eyebrows crinkle when she speaks and the way she holds her hands at her waist, one resting in the cup of the other, when she talks with customers. Ace recognizes her as someone he has seen in the restaurant before, but not as a waitress. Then, she seemed to be running the place.

"I'm Faye-Marie," she says as she passes out menus. "How're y'all?"

"We're fine," Ace says. "Aren't you the owner of this place?"

"Half owner with my sister, Donna. I'm helping wait today because we're short."

"Well, good to see you," Ace says. "I'm Ace Sinclair and this is J'nelle Reade. How are *you* doing?"

"I'm still here," she says, "on God's good earth, and that's saying a lot."

"Amen to that," Ace says.

"Yes," J'nelle says. "Double amen."

Faye-Marie pours them water, then uses the hem of her apron to wipe a spot the cleaning rag missed from the edge of the table. They order quickly, as the lunch menu is small.

"Y'all be good. I'll be back with your wine," she says.

J'nelle begins to talk slowly and deliberately in what strikes Ace as an effort to provide a counterweight to the hardship she talked about over breakfast. She talks about her life: first the Peace Corps, where she taught first aid and public sanitation in the mountains of Ecuador and Peru; then grad school; followed by work for the State Department on education projects in Kenya and Botswana; and finally, after Seth vanished, as a sort of globe-trotting problem-solver in, as she puts it, "the service of American capitalism." She pauses only to say, "Thanks," as she takes the wine from Faye-Marie before she can set it down.

Once again—that fine-tuned brain and hyper-active memory. Ace listens at first and then lets the words flow over and around him.

"At least in those jobs," she says, "I was well paid."

"Is that why you went to Paris in September," he says, "on one of those jobs?"

"To wind one up," she says, "but mostly because I love Paris. Almost all my work now is pro-bono work for refugees."

"In the U.S.?"

"All over."

And suddenly, it's as if the student council president of old has pulled up a chair to the table. The food arrives; J'nelle doesn't notice. She launches into the horrors of worldwide immigration policy, the suffering she witnessed of malnourished children in Africa, the brutality of dictatorships, oppression of women everywhere, and Americans' lackadaisical attitude toward it all. He nods—"Uh huh ... Really ... Yeah ... No doubt." She glances out the window as she spits out the words. "Cruel ... stupid ... racist ... self-defeating ... un-Christian." It continues through lunch and two glasses of wine for her, one for him. When she finally bangs a fist on the table, he taps on her wine glass with a spoon.

"I thought we were staying in the moment."

"I'm sorry. I don't know why I let this get to me, but it does."

"Perhaps it hits close to home."

"Maybe so."

She turns at last to her food amid the soft clinks of silverware and the murmur of conversations at other tables and picks about the edges of her salad. It is like watching a bird drink water. At last, she raises her wine glass, lets it dangle between her thumb and fingers, and looks at him. He feels a sudden urge to grab hold of something.

"Do you believe in God?" she asks.

"No."

"I knew you'd say that."

"So, why did you ask?"

She starts to take a drink, then sets the wine glass down and turns to look out the window at the small harbor as if some hint of what she is searching for is out there among the swaying hulls and riggings.

"I guess I was hoping you did," she says.

"Do you?"

"I'm not sure."

"Does this have something to do with our being seventy-five?" he says.

"Seventy-six."

"OK, seventy-five for me, seventy-six for you—both of us cresting the last wave of middle age."

"Probably, but I've asked myself that question most of my life."

She takes a sip of wine and once again dangles the glass, swinging it pendulum-like back and forth, then turns back to the view out the window.

"Do you remember that Christmas Eve after the candlelight service at Saint Michael's when we were making out in your car and the cops showed up?"

"I remember we did a lot of making out," he says. "The dates and locations are not so clear. My mind was usually focused elsewhere."

He expects at least a smile, an acknowledgment of humor, but when she turns to him, her gaze goes deep into the windows of his eyes.

"It began with us going parking on that shadowy street in Old Town where somebody had broken the streetlamp with a rock or something. It was around midnight, and the cops pulled up beside us with their red light flashing and got out and shined their flashlights all over us and the car before I could get your letter sweater pulled back over my unbuttoned blouse. They demanded our names, and then one of them, a short, square looking guy named Reggie or something, with no neck and not much older than we were, puffed up like a bantam rooster and launched into a sermon about the sins of the flesh and how the devil was sitting there on the dashboard with his pitchfork and dangling tail, watching us and grinning. Do you remember that?"

"Vaguely. I remember looking down at the keys dangling from the ignition and praying you wouldn't say something back."

"He went on and on," she says, "about coveting each other and 'knowing' each other in a sinful way, especially forbidden touching. 'Dirty fingers,' he called it. A creepy feeling came over me that he was relishing the lustful details."

"I do recall that he seemed a little weird," Ace says, "and that at some point you muttered something like idiot and retard under your breath and I started trying to humor him and get it over with."

"Yes, he was weird," she says, "and he got even weirder, remember? He asked our ages, and I said seventeen and you said sixteen. He shined his flashlight in my face and said something like, 'Seventeen, huh! I got a sister who's seventeen, and you look a lot older than that to me.' And then he shined his flashlight all over me like I was a snake or something, and shined it on you and asked if your parents knew you were out with an older woman—he actually used that term—and told you how it was dangerous for your soul and could lead to everlasting damnation. We would both burn in the hottest part of Hell."

Her face is flushed and tense in that way it used to get in high school when something upset her. She is back there now, he thinks, at the hot center of that cold Christmas Eve night. Her fingers fidget around the base of her wine glass as it sits on the table.

"I guess I didn't remember the flashlight assault," he says. "It sounds awful."

"It was awful."

"They finally left though, right? And we moved on."

"No," she says. "His partner rolled his eyes and walked back to their squad car and opened the door and said, 'Come on Reggie, let's go.' But Reggie stood there and kept shining that flashlight on us but mostly on me until I slid down in the seat to get it off me. His chest heaved and his breathing got deeper and faster, and I realized he was sure we'd been having sex, and it turned him on, and that his sermon had really been about him and his own wicked thoughts. He had twisted religion and the Bible into some sort of mental self-abuse."

She takes an unconscious sip of wine, sets the glass down, and looks at him. The flush is gone, and a cryptic smile tugs at those tightly pressed lips. When he saw that smile in high school, he could never be sure what it meant, except that he knew it wasn't joy or amusement.

Disgust maybe. But a slight quiver in it now tells him it means even more than that.

"J'nelle, I'm really sorry that happened, truly. I don't remember it nearly as well as you do, and I can see why it stayed with you. But if it's so unpleasant, why bring it up?"

"Do you remember what happened next?"

"I remember the other cop saying something like, 'That's enough, Reggie,' and taking his arm and dragging him back to their squad car, and they began to jaw at each other, and we drove away."

"Yes. They finally let us go, and you drove away with that red light still flashing through the rear window of the car. It was like it was following us, following me. And with every blink of it came a huge flash of shame, and then anger so that I began to shake. That creep! What right did he have? And you put your hand on mine, and I took it and squeezed it, and it was like you were pulling me out of the hell he had cast me into with his wandering flashlight and dirty little mind."

Ace was never aware he had had that kind of effect on her, ever: rescuer, source of comfort by the mere touch of his hand.

"I did that?" he says.

Her smile is gone now. There is a new eagerness in her eyes.

"Yes, you did. And it rescued me from the burn that flashlight had left on me. It took me back to all the good things we had before Reggie came along with his stupid sermon and heavy breathing: my belief in God,

St. Michael's and Reverend Epps and his civil rights work and all the youth group stuff we did together—in fact everything we did together, including all the lovey-dovey and making out. And there we were, alone once again in your car, silently moving through the quiet streets. It felt like a refuge, it felt so warm and close."

He can almost feel the breathy warmth of the car's dark interior as it carried them through the Christmas Eve night, hear the tinny rattle of the fan in the car's foot heater, smell the butt-slick vinyl seats. Yes, so warm and close, and yet he had had no idea what was going on in the head of the girl next to him with her fingers wrapped in his, though he must have seen and heard everything she did, everything this older J'nelle has just described: the fire-breathing sermon; the wandering flashlight beam; the heaving, uniformed chest; the red light from the cop car flashing in his rearview mirror as he drove away. Had he ever seen what was in her head? And how about her feelings, like the ones she just shared from that night? Did he ever have a clue?

He unlocks his fingers from their grip on the seat of his chair and interlaces them before him on the table in as relaxed a manner as possible, then looks up at her waiting eyes and clears his throat.

"And I kind of just sat there."

"Well yes, but what else could you do?"

"No. I mean afterward, when we were driving away. After it was over."

Once again her gaze drifts out the window.

"Things really are a blur for you," she says.

"Does that upset you?"

"A little."

He waits for her to turn back to him. When she doesn't, he says:

"Was this the night of the cemetery? I remember once we wound up there very late."

"Yes," she says. She's looking at him now. "We passed back by St. Michael's, where we'd just been to the candlelight service and where not more than an hour before I had been so caught up in that starry-eyed vision of us and God and the church, and it seemed as if we'd come full circle. We'd come back to something that was even more than it was before. I moved across the seat and pressed very close, and I think it was at that moment I began to understand for the first time what being in love might mean."

Yes, he thinks, that's it. It was there in that moment and a few others like it. And that's what his dream of the red-winged blackbirds is about, the bright flashes of black, red, and yellow, rising from the marsh. And then they are gone, leaving an emptiness behind them that is a palpable expression of the deepest tenderness. A tenseness that has built in him gives and releases a tidal pool of warmth that flows all over him.

"We were in Old Town by then," he says. "St. Michael's was on the edge of it."

"Yes," she says, "we came to the Old Town Cemetery, and the gates were open, and I caressed your thigh and said let's go in there. Before that evening I would never have done that, never have been the one to make the overture. It just happened."

He remembers now the slow, nimble movement of her hand onto his leg, leading him deftly onward to wherever she was taking them. From that moment, everything seemed perfectly timed. He relaxed his grip on the steering wheel and let his wrist drape over the hard hoop of plastic, James Dean style, tapped his worn brakes, down-shifted—third, second, first—felt the wheel's smooth turn as the car's bald tires veered into the graveyard driveway.

"I've often wondered," she says, "whether you had any idea what was going on in my mind then."

"I knew," he says, "we were not turning into the cemetery to pay our respects to the dead."

She turns again to look out the window. It's as if she's stepped from the restaurant and gone to walk among the rocking boats.

"It was to pay respects to life—or at least to life as I saw it and hoped it would be."

She folds her hands before her on the table and begins to twirl her thumbs. He watches them go round and round, stifles the twitch in his thumbs to do the same.

She glances up at him. "A teenage dream," she says, "huh?"

"Yes," he says, "I guess. But whatever it was, it went very deep. That night it was real, wasn't it?"

"Yes," she says, "it was."

She locks her gaze on him, then drops it to her slowly twirling thumbs. He thinks of a reel winding something in.

"As I recall," she says, "it began with our usual heavy make out in the back seat, but the usual wasn't going to be enough for that night, not for the way I was feeling. And the back seat wasn't either. So I stripped off everything under my dress and took your hand and led you off into the cemetery. It was Christmas Eve, for God's sake, and I was practically naked and barefoot as if I was going to my own infant baptism rather than to get myself deflowered. And we came to this tall obelisk stone with the name Alton Zebulon Fitts on it in fancy script—you remember that? I'll never forget it, he'd been mayor or governor or something—and I knelt on the grave and pulled you down to me."

"I don't remember Zebulon," Ace says, "but I remember that. It was like being drawn into a solemn rite."

The details of the scene come back to him like a jigsaw puzzle where the pieces don't quite fit. But he can feel the intensity of the scene build around him now, as it did then, when she pulled him slowly and surely into the timeless hollow of that evening. Usually in their making out, he was the initiator and the leader-on. But that evening it was different, very different.

He starts to twirl his own thumbs and feels the arthritic knuckles bump and hang on each other. What unfolded between them was so much more than he had ever imagined: not just the sudden eagerness in her body, its new insistence, it was the way it happened once it began, the lightning fast, achingly slow ease of it, the way every movement slid easily into the next as his hesitation folded and skittishness melted away.

He lifts his eyes from his twirling thumbs and risks a quick glance.

A blush has deepened along the ridges of her cheeks and adds a new luster to her eyes, which seem to glow from the darkness around Alton Zebulon Fitts's grave. A memory returns—the feeling of her body under him on the frozen winter earth. Her body felt harder and stronger than usual and lit with energy, yet more tender and yielding. It came at him and faded at the same time.

"Jesus, J'nelle," he says. "This is not fair."

Her thumbs stop twirling and slowly his do too, and he feels the twitch that has been working in the muscle between the base of his thumb and knuckle of his index finger.

It's all quite clear now. The blur of their times together is no longer a blur. This night was the night that decided it all, whatever was going to happen with them. This was the night. Surely, some part of him knew that, somewhere under all the lust and longing and fumbling of hands. Surely, and yet...

"I remember it being very cold," he says, "even for December."

"Yes, it was cold! As you may recall, I was on the bottom."

"And I was probably a bit fumbling and awkward."

A slight smile. "I would agree with that."

"And as I recall, we were almost there, most of the way home, and who stopped it?"

"It wasn't me," she says.

Her eyes are still on him, or maybe on that boy in the graveyard.

"I guess," he says, "the altar boy stepped forth. He got in the way a lot back then."

"I didn't see him," she says. "I saw a cautious boy who didn't want to get his girlfriend pregnant."

Was that it—careful Ace, considerate Ace, wise, prudent Ace? Or was he afraid of taking a step beyond that easy, trance-like world he knew—afraid of her sudden, wild insistence, of where it might lead, of everything?

He looks down at his lifeless hands, resting on the table, waiting for the next current to hit from a Pearlman Shake.

"So when that happened," he says, "when I balked at the starting gate, how did you feel?"

"Disappointed, I guess. Probably a little relieved, and..."

"What?"

"Deflated."

"Deflated?"

"Yes. The whole unity thing: us and our happy-ever-after future, my starry-eyed vision of the Divine, and how it would all come together in some magical never-never land. I think that's when I really began to question that vision. My beliefs had been so strong, but so were those of a lot of people, even a pervert like

Reggie. And my ideas of God and sex seemed about as confused as his. Once you start to ask those questions at that age, it leads to one end."

"Sorry," he says. "I guess I should have screwed your brains out."

"Ha!" she says. "Or vice versa. But it doesn't really matter. That awakening would have happened sooner or later anyway, probably sooner. I was tired of being trapped in my own head."

"Yeah, I guess it would have," he says. "It does for most thinking people."

"That's a tragedy isn't it?" she says.

"Is it?"

"It didn't seem like it then, but now, I don't know."

Her eyes stay on him as he glances up at her and then looks about to catch Faye-Marie's eye and ask for the check.

"I'm getting this," J'nelle says, and reaches into her jeans for her card.

"Not on your life," he says, repeating her phrase from when she rejected his offer of air fare. When Faye-Marie comes with the check, he holds out his credit card without examining the bill.

"You're mighty trusting," Faye-Marie says.

"You look as trustworthy as anyone I've ever met," Ace says.

"That's nice of you to say," she says. "But be careful. There are plenty of folks on this island that aren't. It didn't used to be that way, but since the drugs came in, a lot has changed."

The image of the young mother's face in the grocery store flashes in his mind, the one he gave the water to: wasted, graying skin; cornered eyes.

Faye-Marie gives him a pat on the hand and turns toward the checkout station.

"I like her," says J'nelle. "She reminds me of Mrs. Beacham, our old algebra teacher. Remember her?"

"I remember she gave me a C and chewed me out over it."

J'nelle's fingers are spread wide on the table, and it occurs to him for the first time that the silver band around her finger, the one that looks like the work of an amateur silversmith who was into Celtic art, is probably her wedding band. How could he have missed that? He's been looking at those remarkable fingers ever since she arrived.

Faye-Marie drops the check folder with his card on the table.

"Are y'all going to leave before the hurricane?"

"Probably tomorrow morning," he says.

"A lot of folks have already left. That's why we have such a small crowd today."

"Yes," Ace says. "I've been noticing it's kind of sparse."

Faye-Marie glances from him to J'nelle and back as if she's arrived at a judgment about whether they can be trusted with insider information.

"I'm not sure it's going to hit."

"Why's that?"

"My uncle, Ike Haskell, is the pastor over at the A.M.E. Zion Church on Ocean Drive." She pauses, a slight twinkle of mirth. "He calls it the Lifeboat Holiness Church, but he takes that sign down when the bishop comes. Anyway, Ike was born and raised here. He's been watching hurricanes all his life, and his prediction is that this one's going north of us, up the coast. He predicted the last two they warned us about weren't going to hit, and he was right. And the one before that, he said it was going to hit, and it did. Wiped out that old marina down at the point, bunch of those overbuilt homes along the beach. Cut a new inlet below Mayok Woods. So for right now, I'm relying on Uncle Ike. But if it hits, well, I'll probably stay anyway. Lots to do here. Folks are going to need help."

Ace scans the Visa receipt, adds a generous tip and gives it back to her.

"Thanks," he says. "Your uncle sounds like a smart man."

"He listens to the Lord," Faye-Marie says. She takes the signed check and gathers up their plates.

"Y'all take care now," she says, "and stay safe." Then over her shoulder as she walks away: "And may you be blessed."

"Thank you," Ace and J'nelle say in unison.

When Faye-Marie is out of hearing, Ace says, "I've kinda overlooked that part of it."

"You mean, the folks who won't leave, or can't, the ones she's staying to help?"

"Yes."

"I guess when you've got roots here and family and have made a life here, it's harder to leave."

"When it's your home," Ace says, "leaving is kind of like dying."

She gives him a quick glance. Her lips part to speak, but she presses them together instead, then presses them harder and drops her eyes.

He gives her a tap on the wrist.

"Back to your questions on God and lost faith: have you tried going to church?"

"Yes. What I'm looking for is not there—at least, I can't find it."

"Meditation? Spiritual retreats in the Arizona desert? Pilgrimages to holy sites? Buying a Labrador retriever?"

"I've tried all except the Lab. The closest I came was about six months ago on a trip to South Africa. I got invited to a Zulu wedding celebration. It was outdoors, after the quieter rituals of stepping over the broom and exchange of vows were observed. People were dressed in bright-colored dashikis, turbans, flowing gowns, even animal skins for the groom and a few dignitaries. There was lots of ritual dancing, much of it acting out the coming together of two souls in matrimony. It seemed chaotic at first, then it began to sway to its own rhythm, and the rhythm fused a community that seemed to melt into one being."

She pauses and gives her head a slight shake of embarrassment.

"Seems new agey, I know, but I'm not sure quite how else to say it. Anyway, it pulled me in, not to the dancing—I was on the periphery of the ceremony as part of a circle of guests—but emotionally. It was moving in a joyful, gathering-in sort of way. I felt—again, I don't know how else to say it—a connectedness with the dancing and singing people, with the whole scene. It stirred up a deep spiritual longing."

Her eyes take on a gleam of excitement. She focuses them on the reflection the window makes in the inch of white wine remaining in her glass.

"I assumed it would soon fade away," she says, "but it hasn't. And now I understand that it's been there all along. It's a part of me that I forgot about while I was running all over the world trying to save everything. To make up for not being able to save those dearest to me." She glances up at him. "Hence my question about your belief in God."

"Sorry I wasn't a better help."

"It was an unfair question. I'm just floundering about. I'm not even sure what I'm looking for."

"I'm guessing there aren't many Zulu marriage celebrations around your neighborhood in New York."

"No."

"You could always move to Africa, post a big dowry, snare a husband, and have your own ceremony."

She looks him in the eye again and mouths, "Fuck you," those prim lips, forming precisely around each word, dwelling slightly on the latter as if slowly letting it go.

"I shouldn't have said that," he says. "It was crude and stupid."

He raises his unused soup spoon off the tablecloth and lets it drop with a soft thud.

"Come on," he says. "I want to show you something."

Saturday afternoon

He drives them back to the beach where they walked earlier and pulls Pam's spare binoculars from the glove compartment. They follow the trail over the dunes to the beach and head in the opposite direction than before, southward, past more fishermen. The air seems heavier now, more saturated with the primal odors of the sea. Booms of the surf echo against the violet undersides of thickening, gray clouds.

They leave the beach and turn back across the dunes and bending sea oats to a large wetland that runs from the dunes to a faraway line of woods. Onyx-colored water spreads among bright green skeins of duckweed and water lilies and disappears into drying stands of cattails around the edges. The scene looks bright and slightly luminescent under the gloomy sky. They use the binoculars to find egrets and herons and one roseate spoonbill and at the far end of the marsh, a great horned owl sitting on a snag, its neck and chest feathers rising and twitching in the wind.

"I didn't know owls ate fish," she says.

"They don't," he says. "It's picked an odd spot to hunt. Marsh rats maybe, young nutria."

He lowers the binoculars. "Let's sit."

They find a sandy spot near the top of a dune and sit quietly for a few moments to observe the marsh.

"I don't believe in God," he says, "but when I'm in places like this, I feel something that seems eternal."

"Hmmm," she says. "You mean in nature."

"Special places in nature, like this. The sensation comes on slowly and grows until it becomes very strong. It's like a sense of God."

"Do you feel it a lot?"

"No, and I'm not sure why I feel it sometimes and not others, except that something catches my eye that seems like a signal, a tap on the shoulder or a bell tolling. Like, for example, that owl."

He hands her the binoculars.

"See where the wind catches that little tuft of feathers and lifts it up from that otherwise perfect, speckled breast, not more than three or four feathers, and they hang there and twitch. Not another thing on that owl is moving, not even its head, and yet that bird is keenly aware of everything in this marsh. It's as if, even if I'd never heard of owls, that image has been in my consciousness forever waiting for the right moment to show itself—a perfect embodiment of, of what I don't know, but perfect."

"And you see that owl, with its tuft of feathers lifted by the wind, as a glimpse of God?"

"I *feel* that owl and its tuft of feathers as a suggestion of God, not quite a belief, more a confirmation of yearning." He pauses. "Sort of like your Zulu dance."

She takes another look through the binoculars and lowers them to her lap.

They sit for a moment in silence. The owl shifts slightly on the branch.

"After I leave the place," he says, "I feel this deep sense of gratitude. And I ask myself: gratitude to whom, to what?"

She says in a half-whisper: "Who was it said that if God did not exist, we'd have to invent Him?"

"Voltaire."

"Wow! Impressive," she says.

"I'm not sure where I dug that up."

"So, is that what we are doing—making up our own version of God?"

"I have no idea."

They sit for a while in silence until he scoops up sand in his fist and releases it slowly over her foot and watches it run between her toes.

"Nice," she says. "What brought that on?"

"I don't know. A token, I guess. Maybe a baptism."

A pair of blackbirds has arrived at the far end of the marsh to harass the owl. Ace pushes himself to his feet and nods toward the circling, diving blackbirds. "They'll stay after him until he leaves," he says. "Apparently, they have a different view of him than I do."

He extends his hand to help her up.

As they walk back to the car, the wind whistles in their ears and skitters stinging pellets of sand against their ankles. Waves rush in to slosh about their feet. Some of the fishermen have given up fighting the surf and left the beach. A man and woman, in an SUV with six surf rod holders attached to its roof bars, drive past them, eyes focused straight ahead. The SUV's fat tires make a scrunching sound on the sand.

At the parking area, Ace's car, a Subaru old enough to have a straight drive transmission, is the only car left. They keep their silence, as if the serenity of the marsh has followed them down the beach.

The road home runs along the narrow isthmus between the sound on one side and soaring dunes on the other. The car floats along as if carrying the day and the things they have done, and Ace floats along with them. His mind runs back to that night in high school, when they were in his car driving away from the two cops, and she was across the seat from him before she moved close, and he just sat there behind the wheel and everything he did not know in the whole wide world sat on the seat between them.

BACK AT THE house, J'nelle excuses herself for a nap. Ace finds an old Peter Matthiessen novel, *Far Tortuga*, and climbs to the roof deck. Beyond the dunes, white-capped, gray-green waves surge toward the beach, throwing off strings of soapy spray that blow ahead of them in the wind. Regardless of Faye-Marie's Uncle Ike's prediction, this storm is not going to veer north. He's almost sure of it.

A pessimist, Pam called him. *There's a proper time for pessimism; it can save your ass.*

After a few minutes of trying to control his book's flapping pages, he gives up. He goes out to his tool shed, finds his hedge-trimmer, and goes to work on the beach hollies that have overgrown the back steps. Clip, snip, snip—tough bushes. His mind soon wanders to the woman napping in his guest bedroom, who sat across the table from him at lunch with her swinging wine glass, the light through the window lighting her features, and the meaning in what she said weaving in and out of her words, staying just beyond his reach. She's an ace at complicating things; she always was.

And that story about them making out in the graveyard: he's not sure it happened exactly the way she told it, but like the sight of the red-winged blackbirds rising in his dream, it stirred an excitement in him that bled into an infinite tenderness. And the other sensations, the cold earth and night air, the movement of her body under him, all seemed so strong when she told the story. Was she naked under her dress? He would have remembered that, wouldn't he? But she was sure of it, and she looked him straight in the eye when she told him, and her lips were not tense or pressed but relaxed like they used to be when he bent to kiss her.

He pauses his clipping. For the first time since he can remember, an erection pushes at the front of his pants.

Sweet Jesus. That cannot be what this is about.

An old feeling returns, a sense of suddenly being alone in the midst of things going on around him. It used to happen when he was a lawyer trying a case, right in the middle of the courtroom when he was cross examining a witness or making an objection or arguing to the jury. He stepped out of himself and became a silent spirit, watching what he was doing.

Those were times when he often made mistakes—asked a witness one too many questions on cross examination, brought a witness to tears, objected to a piece of favorable evidence he should have let in. Lost a case he might have won.

Maybe he's screwing up now. Maybe he screwed up when he asked her down here. The graveyard story unsettled him. It brought back that old feeling of being behind and out-of-step, of her pulling him along, taking them both into something he did not understand, or for that matter, even see. It happened a lot back then—maybe because she was older, smarter, quicker, who knows? And there is some of that feeling now, isn't there, of scrambling, trying to catch up?

He resumes his clipping, that absent part of himself still watching from above.

The case he regrets most from his days as a lawyer still gives him that watched-from-above feeling. But it is not one in which he made mistakes. In fact, he was brilliant; he won a case no other lawyer wanted to touch, a nasty spouse-abuse case, handled the witness for the prosecution just right—like a magician, one observer said, like an ace—trapped her in her own lie. Even as he and his client walked out of the courtroom, he did not feel good about it—not only the result, but what he had done to achieve it. And he did not feel good about what happened next either, between his client and the prosecution witness. It still haunts him, as if his conscience wakes up and begins to pound the walls of his skull with a hammer.

Pam tried to help: "You did nothing wrong, Ace. In fact, you did everything right; you are a very good lawyer, and you did what good lawyers are supposed to do—defend their clients."

He had already told himself that; he's told himself at least a thousand times since, and it's got nothing to do with anything, especially what happened in that case.

And the woman asleep right now in his guest bedroom, who watched her husband disintegrate before her eyes, who ruined her own chance to have kids, who lost not only her husband but her adopted daughter, just watched them slip slowly away—might she understand how he feels about that case?

And if she did, what difference would it make to him? What difference, when he gets right down to it, does she herself make—conjurer of graveyard memories, or are they graveyard tales?

Saturday evening

He hears her stirring, returns the clippers to the shed, and goes to the kitchen to chop asparagus to go with the cuts of grouper he plans to cook for supper. When she exits the bedroom and shuts the door, it sounds like the final click in something and the opening bell to something else.

She has changed from jeans into another flowing, ankle-length skirt and a black turtle-neck that sets off the reddish tones in her features, slightly puffy from sleep. Yet another set of finely crafted earrings dangles at the edge of her hair to catch late day light.

"You look nice," he says.

She stops across the kitchen island counter from him. "Thanks, but I need to warn you that I wake up very slowly from naps, especially after a couple glasses of wine. I may be only partially coherent for a while."

"That's what beach houses are for. Want some more wine?"

"I'll wait until I've emerged from the twilight zone. Why don't you give me something to do? I promise not to cut off a finger."

"Turn on the TV and check on the whereabouts of our friend, Freya. Channel 6."

The channel blinks on to the governor of the state at a lectern, surrounded by first responders and National Guard officers dressed in combat fatigues and standing at parade rest.

"…could build to a monster storm," the governor says, "…potential for serious damage and threat to human life. Do not take this storm lightly. Residents of the counties of Perkins, Holton, Pamunky, Bartow, and Secutan should be prepared to evacuate within the next twelve to twenty-four hours."

"Aren't we in Secutan?" J'nelle says.

"Yes."

"So…?"

"So, if you leave tomorrow morning as planned, you should be fine."

"When do you plan to leave?"

"Probably tomorrow afternoon, depending on how things go. I'll need to pull in the deck furniture, batten the hatches, etc."

The storm report continues with a return to the TV station's map chart with an excited young man standing next to it, flicking his virtual pointer at possible areas of landfall. Pomeiooc Island is near the center of a purple shadow in the shape of a horn of plenty.

She watches for another ten minutes, then wanders out to the porch. The stiff breeze off the ocean slams the screen door shut behind her.

"Wow!" she calls. "Things have picked up."

"Go up to the high deck," he says. "You can get a good view of what the ocean is doing."

He hears her feet on the steps to the upper deck and imagines her standing at the railing while the wind blows her hair off her neck and pulls it tight from her temples and forehead, flaps her long skirt and forms it tight around her hips and legs. He has not let himself imagine what she looks like under her clothes. Old like him, no doubt—saggy, wrinkled skin; things that grow on it; too many bones—but maybe in a special way that cheats age, like she has managed to do with the features of her face and her bare arms and slim fingers.

Once again, that feeling of the football tumbling, falling from his grasp.

"I've gotta stop this," he whispers to himself. "Dial it back."

He coats the grouper with garlic salt (his catchall, generic seasoning), pepper, and olive oil and places it in the oven while he grills the asparagus. Candles—should he light a couple? There are two small purple ones in the pantry, probably scented, and he hates scented candles. So did Pam, so he has no idea how they got in the pantry. Little nets around the base of them—probably a sign they're "votive," whatever the hell that means. Anyway, it smacks of spiritualism of some kind, and he's had enough of that for the day.

He finally locates the stubby remains of two fat white candles in the back of a drawer, sets them on the table, and works the corkscrew on a bottle of pinot noir as he goes to the screen door to call J'nelle to dinner. And there he pauses, one hand holding the wine bottle with the corkscrew stuck in the top and the other holding open the screen door. In spite of the fact that he did most of the heavy cooking when Pam was alive and in spite of the fact that he is the host and J'nelle the guest, he has a nagging feeling of being the domestic manager between them, the server and tender—*Come to supper; supper's ready, dear*—another version of that *I Love Lucy* scene that keeps rerunning through his mind. And J'nelle seems content to stand back and leave it all to him, though she did offer to help—half-heartedly. She's not into it, the hands-on serving and tending part. Well, maybe if they were in her house. No, she'd be taking him out to dinner.

Anyway, why the hell is he letting this bother him?

He calls loudly to make himself heard above the wind.

"Coming," she says, and appears at the top of the weatherworn flight of steps, where she pauses to look down at him.

"You're taking very good care of me," she says.

"Happy to do so."

Yes, actually, he is happy to take care of her, and he hasn't felt that way in a long time.

He waits with the screen door open as she descends the steps and passes through the door. A slight whiff of perfume comes off her. He usually doesn't like perfume on women any more than in candles, but hers has a soft warm smell, like the powdery space of her teenage bedroom that he conjured for himself last night while she got herself ready for bed in the guest bedroom below.

Not really memories, though—images so strong, they seem like memories—the bureau, the smells, the waiting bed, the flex of her naked foot on the soft, plush rug. Images so strong he believes them.

She watches while he slides the fish and asparagus onto the plates and sprinkles slivered almonds and soft goat cheese on the asparagus.

"Nice," she says. "A masterpiece."

They sit and eat slowly, the talk wandering from her work and his days as a lawyer, to his kids. She eats heartily for a change. The silverware clinks loudly on their plates. The unlit candles sit before them on the table like the columns of a long-ago vanished temple.

Shit, he thinks, *I should find some matches and light them.*

J'nelle's fork of grouper stops halfway to her mouth.

"What was Pam like," she says, "if you don't mind?"

He stares at a spot on the table between the two candles that seems vast and barren. The image comes to him of that icy crevasse on the Diamond Peak Glacier, where Seth took his fatal leap. Dark and deep, J'nelle had said, blue-gone-to-black. Exactly, except with Pam, there remains the slightest intimation of blue, of light not quite gone.

"She was smart," he says. "She was a talented painter too, but most of all she was smart. She picked things up out of nowhere. And if it was something she was really interested in, like astronomy or birding, she was an expert at it. All that Jungian stuff about the creative side versus analytical side, right-brain/left-brain, masculine

versus feminine—it was all one in her. It all worked together. She kept her hair in a bowl cut that looked sort
of mannish, but she had a very female kind of wisdom."

"She sounds like a very special woman."

"She was."

"And I'm guessing, athletic."

"Outdoorsy."

"And no bullshit."

"Right, no bullshit."

A tone enters his voice he has not heard since before
Pam died.

"She too did not believe in terms of endearment," he
says, "or at least she didn't practice them."

"Did you?"

"It's hard to do when they flow in only one direction."

From the corner of his eye, he can see J'nelle turning
the stem of her wine glass as if winding a small motor
in her brain.

"For some reason," he says, "she didn't seem to trust
them. I never knew why that was."

He takes a sip of wine. "But it would have been nice."

"Maybe," says J'nelle, "they just didn't come naturally to her."

"Maybe."

J'nelle sips her wine, sets her glass down, and continues to finger the stem. *What does she fidget with*, he wonders, *when there's not a wine glass around?*

She looks at him. "You are still very much in love
with her."

"Yes."

"And when you go alone to those lovely places like the marsh you took me to this afternoon, places where you sense the eternal, she is there."

"Yes, I suppose she is."

"I think she was lucky. I think you both were."

"We were. And then our luck ran out, and she was gone."

Saturday night

They clear the table and put away dishes and silverware in silence. He is keenly aware of her movements even when he is turned away from her toward the sink and dishwasher.

"Do you have some music we could play?" she says.

"I'm hopelessly behind in the Bluetooth revolution, but there's a CD player in the top of that little radio on the counter, and a few old CDs in that drawer. I keep forgetting to bring more."

She opens the drawer, pulls out three CDs and reads the labels.

"*Hot Rocks* by the Rolling Stones; Mozart, Chopin, Debussy, *Music for Meditation and Relaxation*; *A Blues Christmas* by various artists. Interesting collection."

"At least it's eclectic," he says. "Take your pick."

"I'm not quite ready for Mick Jagger, and we haven't even had Halloween yet, so I'm going with the old guys. Chopin and candlelight might be nice."

She places the CD in the player and goes to stand by the dinner table. 'Where do you want these?"

"What?"

"The candles."

"Uh, over there," he says, nodding to the coffee table. He digs a book of matches from another crowded drawer and hands them to her.

She moves the candles, lights them, then slips off her shoes and takes a seat in one of the pillowed chairs, with her legs folded beneath her under the thin curtain of her skirt.

An image pops into his head from long ago—the same quick movement, maybe she was in shorts or a bathing suit, her tanned legs curling, her upper body tilting as she pulled them in.

He brings the wine and glasses, turns on a standing lamp, and sits on the couch at an angle to her chair. Dusk has deepened into night. The lamp casts a soft yellow glow over where they are seated. Strains of "Clair de Lune" drift zephyr-like about the room, and the candles flicker as if touched by the wind whistling in the eaves outside.

"Do you ever wonder," she says, "how your life might have been different if certain things hadn't happened or maybe happened in a different way?"

"Like what, for instance?"

"Lots of things. But since our talk today, I've been thinking how my life might have been different if we hadn't met and gotten close in high school."

"It's hard to extrapolate something like what happened between us and run it forward through the years."

"I suppose so," she says. She begins to pick at the fabric of her skirt. "But maybe that's the wrong question. I think what I really want to know is whether that thing we had in the tender days of our youth, with all its yearnings and intensity of feelings, somehow spread quietly into the rest of our lives. Or is it still back there, frozen in time?"

"Clair de Lune" has given way to a deeper melody—Bach—that conjures moonlit clouds drifting over dark water. Beyond the window, across from where he is seated, the darkness heaves with the approaching storm. He wonders where the owl is and his nightly visitor, the raccoon. He looks back at J'nelle, the way the long bones of her legs shape the skirt as it falls over and away from them.

"All I know," Ace says, "is that sometimes late at night, it doesn't seem very frozen."

"No," she says. "It beckons; it seems alive."

He sets his wine glass on the table and leans forward with his elbows on his knees. A hint of the Pearlman Shake tugs at the tendon in his wrist. It's left him alone most of the day. Why now?

"You know," he says, "I never imagined that what happened back then bothered you in the least after it was over. The way I saw it was, you just left and I was there by myself. And then I left as well."

He gently massages his wrist to stop the shake. The yellow flames of the candle nearest his wine glass reflect deep and bright in the red wine. He lets go his wrist and opens and closes his fingers, stretching and loosening them.

"But not entirely," he says. "Some part of me stayed, and sometimes my mind wanders back there, looking for that boy, with an urge to bring him into the present."

"But he's not there, is he?" she says.

"No, he's there. He just can't come."

As soon as he lifts the wine glass, the shake hits. He steals a glance to see if J'nelle has noticed it. Her gaze flicks deftly from his hand and wine glass to his face.

"That's sad, Ace," she says, "even more than if he wasn't there."

Bach has given way to a Chopin nocturne. The strains come in gentler waves, moving slowly, leaving behind them a wake of silence.

"To be honest," he says, "when my mind wanders back there, I'm probably searching for the young girl too. That is, for you."

"Do you find her?"

"Fleeting images in the rearview mostly, tending toward the pornographic."

She smiles at him across the rim of her wine glass.

"I look for her too," she says. "I look for us. But the more I see of her, the less I like. She was a confused mess."

She unfolds her legs from under her and sits in that almost prayerful pose, elbows on knees, wine glass cupped in her hands. The candlelight flickers over her face. For the first time, he feels its glow on his own.

"I'm sorry," she says. "I didn't mean to lead us down this gloomy path and ruin a nice evening."

He sets the wine glass on the coffee table, rests forward, and grips his trembling hand with the other, squeezing tighter and tighter.

Goddamnit, stop!

"Lost times bring melancholy," he says. "And the music doesn't help."

She straightens in the chair, leans forward, and taps his wrist. "Maybe we could cheer things up by dancing; you were always good at that."

"To Chopin?"

"No. We can put on the Stones."

The shakes have eased, but suddenly the stiffness is there like a hide stretched to dry in the sun—in his knees, hips, thighs, and ankles. A life of sitting, talking, leaning intensely over counsel tables.

"I'm afraid I don't do that anymore," he says.

"Oh."

"And you do?"

"Sometimes at night, when I'm alone."

"Once again," he says, "I'm impressed."

"It helps to cure the blues."

"Well," he says, "speaking of the blues, there are some slower songs on the Christmas CD that still have a nice beat."

"How much slower?"

"Well, slow," he says. "But if you don't want to…"

"It's not that I don't want to…"

"It's just—what?"

She drains the last of her wine, sets the glass on the coffee table and holds out her hand like a nineteenth century debutante.

Her long fingers drape from her knuckles in a

delicate fashion that nevertheless seems slightly claw-like. He wonders how his swollen knuckles, ropey tendons, and wasted flesh feel to her—clumsy, no doubt, maybe even dead. They rise together. Her lips, stained from the wine, are a garish violet in the lamp's slightly greenish glow. He guides her around the coffee table and into an open area of the room, where he leaves her to change the CD to the Christmas blues album, then returns as the chimes begin in Charles Brown's "Please Come Home for Christmas," and they begin to sway slowly, their bodies in the posture of eleven-year-olds at their first dance class: *your arm, Ace, extended shoulder high, palm up and open; your hand, J'nelle, resting lightly upon it; your other hand, Ace, held against the small of her back, like so; and your left hand, J'nelle, resting lightly on Ace's shoulder.*

A tremor runs from his elbow to his wrist and sends a dull current to the bones of the hand he holds to cradle hers. There is no way she doesn't feel it. Her head is canted slightly to the side, looking at what he cannot tell. The objects in the room—his grandfather's heavy wooden desk and matching swivel chair, still smelling vaguely of pipe smoke; a recliner and side table holding a shaded reading lamp; a throw rug; a stack of split live oak by the fireplace—seem withdrawn into the shadows, away from the slow beat of the music and Charles Brown's soulful voice, pleading for his love to come home for Christmas.

The song ends with a chiming fade, and the next song begins: Eartha Kitt's "Santa Baby." Their feet stop their slow shuffle.

"Doesn't really work," he says.

Her head is still turned toward the side, her face lowered now, eyes on the floor. Her hand begins to slip from his shoulder. Her other hand, still laid lightly in his, will surely slip away as well. Then everything seems to pause. He presses his hand softly into her back and she moves quickly and without effort against him, featherlight. Her hair brushes his neck. Her wild honey smell comes deep and rich in the dimly lit room.

They are caught in that old pattern of touch, anchored by the press of the top of her head against his jaw. And then she does that thing she used to do that melted the space between them and transfigured everything, that erased time: that soft sigh of her body into his. The room around them and everything in it, the squeal of the wind around the eaves and distant boom of the surf fade away, and it is just the two of them holding each other, turning slowly in the shadows.

She squeezes his shoulder tighter, pulls him even closer, and lowers her head to rest against his chest.

The song ends, and a new one—Dodie Steven's "Merry Christmas Baby," begins. She melts into him even more, holding tighter, and then suddenly her arms relax and she steps away. Her gaze drops to the floor between their feet.

"I didn't intend this when I came down here," she says, "really."

"I don't know what I intended anymore," he says.

Dodie's song ebbs and flows through her make-believe Christmas day: her lover with someone new, but still sending him a card wishing they were close. There's an ache in it, tears running through a lilting voice.

Ace and J'nelle begin to sway slightly, but she keeps her distance.

"I don't know what to do now," he says.

Her hand slides from his shoulder down his arm. She entwines her fingers in his and, with the tip of her thumb, lightly strokes a tendon on the back of his hand.

"Is there a graveyard somewhere nearby?" she whispers.

His erection begins to stir. Those memories she keeps whispering back to life right in front of him—the cotillion, the scene with the cops, the cemetery where she lay on her back on the grave as he lowered himself onto her and pressed them both into the earth, those memories are like fellow dancers snuggling against them, nudging him closer into the warmth she has created.

But there is that other thing: he did not talk with Pearlman about sex, he never imagined, never let himself, not really, and so, well, what is next?

She rests back on her heels. Her face is in deep shadow, but he can feel the teasing smile.

"You don't have to worry about me getting pregnant this time," she says.

Sweet Jesus.

"Well, actually," he says, "there is a grave, a bunch of them, early Native Americans, in the grove behind the house, but the exact location is uncertain, and you know, there's a sacred aspect to it."

"I'm only kidding."

"Right," he says. "I just wanted to be sure."

"I mean, about the grave."

It comes to him in a flash that this scene is not unusual for her, sex with a guy over a weekend. She still does it, at least occasionally, with guys she knows or meets. Maybe on the trip she just took, a shared cabin on the ship. Occasional sex; recreational sex. He does not understand those terms. He hasn't been laid since Pam's illness took its turn.

She takes a step back and glances at her empty glass on the coffee table. "I guess I had too much wine. And then the music—those old Christmas songs—and the candles probably didn't help."

He pulls her to him, encircles her waist, and intercepts her lips on their way to rest against his shoulder. Their thinness is so familiar, their quick parting, the hesitant then gently flicking tongue with its lingering taste of wine. His own body vanishes except for the feel of his fingertips on her skin through the finely woven cotton of her turtleneck, the age-softened, slack weight of it, and the long muscles that slide beneath. She presses her whole body into his. She must feel it, surely—his erection hard against her. His hand slips downward from the base of her spine to her rear.

By now another song has started, Ray Charles and Betty Carter's, "Baby It's Cold Outside." One of his favorites, but out of tune with the moment.

"Come," he says, "let's find a better place."

He leads her down the dark hallway to an unoccupied bedroom, the only one in the house in which the bed is made up other than his and the guest bedroom. The room is pitch black. A window, poorly fitted in its casement during the remodel, rattles sporadically in the wind.

"Here," he says and feels his way carefully toward the bed and, when he finds it, guides her to it and pulls her close once more for another kiss that is deeper and more open than the first one, but held maybe a second or two too long. He is hung in his own uncertainty. Movie couples that get to this point either slowly undress each other or tear at each other like badgers, popping buttons, yanking at belt buckles, and stripping off bras. But her top has no buttons and he has no idea where to begin on her skirt.

She ends the kiss by tracing his lips with her tongue, then rests her head under his chin, and they hold each other until finally she takes a step back and pulls her top slowly over her head. He senses—almost feels in the dark—the deft movement of her arms, wrists, and elbows and the slight bend of her head as the garment slips over it and releases her hair and the dangling silver earrings. The bra would be next, that's how Pam used to do it, reaching behind her to unsnap it, then slipping her arms through the straps. Then the skirt, dropping softly to the floor.

"I'm kinda shy about doing this alone," she says.

He fumbles at his belt and gets that sensation he's had before when alone with someone in true, black dark—standing close to them or sitting or squatting, like in a foxhole in Vietnam—that maybe it's all imaginary, maybe the other person is not there and he is alone, in the bedroom or garage or jungle or in some unknown realm of the universe, alone with no one but himself.

He listens for the soft release of her bra, the slip of its straps on her skin, the settling of her dropped skirt upon the floor and cannot hear them above his own breathing. But she is here, next to him—he can feel it like a spirit in the room—slowly taking her clothes off, and in seconds they will stand before each other in the naked darkness, and she will not be a spirit. She will be very, very real.

She finishes undressing ahead of him and stands waiting in the pool of clothing at her feet. When he is free of his own clothes, he freezes for a moment, then turns and holds open the bedspread and sheet.

"Here," he says, and touches her back between her shoulder blades and guides her under the covers, then follows and wraps his arm around from behind and presses her close. Her perfume, buoyed on the smell of warm skin, fills the air around him.

His penis stirs again, and everything seems safe and well and sure there in the darkness, so far from the bright lights and vinyl table of Pearlman's examination room. But something lurks, doesn't it? Some hollow, faceless thing has followed him out of that shiny place all the way to here, and now crouches in the black shadows of the room. He imagines the smell of its breath, sour and hollow, but there is no smell. And there is no breath, like death has no breath.

He kisses her back between her shoulder blades and up her neck.

"Nice," she says, and turns her body toward him. The kissing begins again. She traces a fingertip over the features of his face and then along the five-inch, half-moon scar on his chest. The impulse is sudden and strong to squeeze her and gather in everything that has passed between them and everything that did not pass in those intervening years and mix it all together, reclaim it all as if it had never stopped.

She slips from under his arm and lies on her back with one arm flung above her head and the hand of the other limp over one of her breasts as if guarding it. He goes unsteadily onto his knees, wavers on the springy mattress, and adjusts himself between her open legs, then bends and kisses her cheek and earlobe and neck, the earring dangling light and cool against his lips.

And so yes, he is here now with her, wrapped in the cocoon of this warm darkness—finally! and he will make it, and it will all be fine. It will be complete within this moment.

But that shadowy, faceless thing is still there, breathing now, whispering the metallic acronyms: MRI, CAT, EMG, and mocking Pearlman's buddy-buddy optimism, the smokescreen of words and smiles he spread over the glare from the polished tile floor.

A tremor starts in the arm Ace is using to prop himself and to lower himself to kiss her. The faceless thing's breaths moan and whistle like wind through a cracked-open window. Ace's erection begins to wilt. He considers for a panicked moment the option of taking it in his hand to revive it and then for a fleeting second asking her to. His lips are at her ear. Just a whisper is all it would take. And she would do it happily, he is sure, to consummate that cold Christmas Eve that today at lunch, when she told the story, had felt so close and now is fading back into the murky past.

He pushes himself away and rests back on his heels, bends forward and kisses her softly at the base of her throat, then rests back again. He tries to relax his shoulders, but the tremor won't stop.

"I'm sorry," he says. "It has nothing to do with you. It's all me. You are even sexier than you used to be and a very attractive woman, in every way I can think of."

She lowers her arms to her side, inhales slowly, and releases a long whispery breath.

"It's OK," she says, and places a hand on his arm. "Really, it's OK."

At her touch, the tremor slowly stops. He rolls away from her onto his back and searches the darkness for an outline of the ceiling fan with its unlit globe, listens to the rattle of the window, which seems twice as loud as it did when they came into the room.

He feels only the light touch of her fingers on his arm, and he wants to seize them and press them to his lips, but the urge seems so melodramatic he cannot bring himself to do it. The window rattles and rattles. The approaching storm is like a great, marching army, beating drums and sounding trumpets outside the walls of the house.

"I guess," he says, "maybe we should have tried the graveyard. But I didn't do so well on my first try at that either."

She gives his arm a soft squeeze. "It's the closeness that counts."

She adjusts herself onto her side to face him, head propped in her hand, and trails her fingers slowly back and forth across his wrist.

"Ace, what is the shake about—the one I keep noticing in your wrists and hands."

Maybe now, in the darkness, he sees the vague outline of the ceiling fan; or maybe he's just imagining it because it's like a fan that was in his bedroom when he was a kid.

"Not sure," he says.

"Have you had it checked?"

"I talked to my doctor."

"And?"

"Tests are scheduled next week, a whole alphabet of them."

She rolls onto her back. Her fingers slide from his wrist to his hand and close around it. Her squeeze grows in intensity until he feels a slight ache.

"The main reason I could not come down here before the weekend," she says, "is that I had a biopsy on Thursday. I will get the results next week."

"Where?" he says.

"Breast."

Pam's disease. My aunt's and grandmother's, he thinks. *It inhabits the house.*

135

"One or both?"

"Just the left one for now."

"I'm so sorry," he says.

His mind returns to Pearlman's examination room, the way his lawyer's critical eye sought out objects—color pattern on the vinyl chairs, blue latex fingers emerging from the glove dispenser, the store-brought print of Tuscan wine country on the otherwise blank, colorless wall—to distract himself from the uncertainty that was like a third presence in the room.

"What have they said about it?" he says. "I mean, do they know…"

"…how bad it is?" she says. "My doctor doled out the standard ration of encouragement—caught it early, probably treatable without surgery, etc., etc.,—but I could hear it in her voice: she's just guessing. My age doesn't help. Neither does my distrustful attitude."

"What's next?"

"Who knows? More tests, more waiting, sooner or later maybe a hard decision."

They do not speak. An unnamed pulse beats quietly in the room.

"I would like to be held," she says. "You know, the spoon thing. But please be careful. The biopsy spot is still sore."

Ah, yes, that hand guarding her breast as she offered herself to him. He should have guessed: a spot bandage maybe, a stitch or two. Like Pam's.

They lie in a silent flight of time as the weight of his arm sinks slowly into the hollow between her hip bone and ribs. He rests his cheek and forehead against the top of her back as it curves away from him, that beautiful back he saw at the reunion, naked in the hot light of the mid-afternoon sun. Suddenly there is her body only—not her bony hips and sagging stomach, the withered breasts or the specter of age—but the warm, fleshy length of her from her toes to the top of her head, with her slowly thumping heart. It is all one in this person snuggled into him in this baby-like closeness, and his body is there as well, not lost and wasted but alive and holding on, pressing her close. And time is short, and this closeness—he could never get enough of it.

She begins to cry in soft muffled sobs, like sleep sounds, and the more he hears them, the more they seem a prelude to a long, aching keen. It is a mother's sound, a cry of ever-searching love.

Saturday around midnight

He wakes when she takes his hand to her lips, then presses it against her chest.

Her breathing is calm, but there is a hint of agitation like the one he sensed in high school just before that wild version of her, the one he called Midnight J'nelle, appeared with a wild idea, like spying on the Klan rally or skipping the last day of school. Once they made boilermakers with bourbon she stole from her parents' liquor cabinet. It was the sickest he'd ever been.

She gives his fingers a soft squeeze.

"How would it be," she says, "if we went out to the beach for a midnight swim?"

"Now?"

"Yes, now. The night is still young."

"Midnight is not young."

"It can be. It's all in the mind."

He waits in the fanciful hope that she is joking, then says, "It's rough out there, J'nelle, even for an ex-swimming champ."

"It should be OK if we stay close to shore."

"And cold. The water has cooled over ten degrees in the last month."

"Seth's parents had a place on Nantucket. I'm used to it. Besides, I need to get into water, real natural water from the depths of the ocean, full of salt and flakes of kelp and darting, frightened fish. I need to feel it around me."

"You really want to go out in this wind and do that?"

She raises his fingers to her lips. "I want to do that with you."

He rises from the bed, finds the wall switch by the door, and flicks on the light.

"No," she says, "leave it off. Please."

They put on their underwear, and she waits in the dark hallway while he takes two large beach towels from the linen closet and pulls a sweatshirt from the drawer in his room. He hands the sweatshirt to her and waits while she puts it on. Then he wraps one of the towels about her, chin to toe, before she steps into the lamplit area in the main room.

He follows, wrapping his own towel about him. She pauses in the lamplight and turns.

"Could we have a sip of something first?

"Sure. I'll open a new bottle. Red or white?"

"Have you got something more the color of brandy or Scotch?"

"Both, but that might not be a good idea before we take on this ocean. The wine either, for that matter."

"I'll take a finger of Scotch and save the brandy for later."

He pours two one-finger glasses of Scotch. She stands with the towel clutched to her chin and one arm poking out to take the Scotch, then holds out her glass to his.

"Cheers!"

A light clink of the glasses.

"Cheers," he says, and thinks but does not say, *We who are about to die salute you.*

Between the two swallows she takes to down her Scotch, she watches him sip his. On her slightly swollen lips, the hint of a smile.

"Why are you doing this?" he says.

"You mean what we did this evening or the entire visit or the midnight swim idea?"

"I meant the midnight swim idea, but maybe the question applies to all of it."

"Let's don't try to answer those questions now. Maybe they will answer themselves."

His glass still has a sip or two of Scotch in it. She takes it from him, sets it on the counter, then takes his hand.

"Maybe it will all come clear in the bosom of the deep blue sea."

"It ain't blue," he says.

They descend the front porch steps to the yard. The wind blows over and around the maritime forest barrier to the east in heavy gusts and whips their towels so hard Ace and J'nelle drop each other's hand and hug themselves to prevent the towels from blowing away. They weave their way across the yard and into the dunes, where he takes their towels and her sweatshirt and stuffs them under a craggy piece of driftwood. She watches with her arms hugged to her chest, then suddenly begins to strip off her panties and bra.

"Here," she says. "I doubt they'll make much difference, even if they stay on in those waves."

He strips off his underwear, and takes her hand as they step from the dunes onto the beach. Out there in the darkness, the massive waves rise, throw off spume and boom upon the shore in an angry, brutal way. The wind comes even harder and he feels even more naked. Retreating waves rake the sand from beneath his feet. She staggers against him, tightens her grip on his hand, and kisses the top of his shoulder.

"Let's go," she says.

"Are you sure?"

"Yes, but please don't let go of me unless I say so."

He wades in first, leading her. The water is cold and full of broken seaweed and bits of shells that sting his legs and feet. Rushing waves smack his shins, splash up to his crotch, pitch into his stomach. He feels her falter and tighten her grip.

He turns and yells over the wind.

"You want to go back?"

"No, I want it all over me."

He thinks of rip currents and undertow, usually more of a problem up the beach where the shore is less protected, but this is not a usual time. The water rises to his chest and pulls even harder against him in its outward rush than it does when it rushes in. He lurches about, loses her hand, and has to turn and do a small dive to recover it. He has not been in the ocean in a couple of years, and he is weaker now in his legs and upper body, his balance all but gone. And what about the Pearlman Shake? Maybe cold salt water will help keep it at bay.

He can feel the next wave building out there in the darkness, a rolling, watery barrel muscled by the sea. The swell that precedes it lifts him off his feet. Once again, she slips away, and this time there is no finding her. He is up to his neck, fighting to get himself vertical and his feet planted before the wave hits. Then suddenly she is there next to him, finishing her last free style stroke in that smooth way he remembers. It always seemed so effortless for her, not challenging the water but slipping eel-like through it.

"We should go back," he shouts. "This is too much."

She throws her arm across his chest and grips his shoulder, then pulls him to her just as the wave breaks against them, smack into his chest, and she is gone and he is tossed end-over-end. His back and shoulders grind into the gritty bottom. He fights to push himself upright and find her before the counter rush comes. But there is no bottom, and he feels himself moving sideways and slightly seaward down the beach, then suddenly faster, away from shore, then much faster, a sensation of being sucked into the sea.

This is it, this is a rip current, and damn it all, he knew the danger and ignored it so that whatever started between them, back there in that confection of candlelight and music, could continue. And to where, for God's sake? He should have stopped it. An old man, trying to prove what?

And where in the name of God is she?

The current hauls him away into the seething sea, choking him with mouthfuls of salty water faster than he can spit them out. Everything they did earlier is now fading. Everything else in his life is fading—kids, grandkids, old friends—drifting away into their own lives, and he is not there.

And those memories of Pam—if he dies, do they die with him?

A big swell washes over him as the current from the shore continues to push him out.

He cannot leave all of that behind; he cannot just let it go. And so, first you don't panic—right? You go with the current, let it take you away from shore. And then somehow you turn and swim parallel to the shore—or is it at an angle away from the shore? And then you turn again in sort of a hook and swim toward the shore. But how far out do you go before you make that final turn and go for it? In this storm-driven water, how do you do all of that?

And J'nelle, does she know any of this? That green, yellow, and blue diagram, magneted to the door of his fridge, of how to escape a rip current, he should have showed it to her.

He should have thought for once; he should have said, "No! And no! And no!" And "Goddamnit no!"

The wind hits in great gusts that whip strings of salt water and snot from his face and hair. He gulps a breath before another swell hits.

There is a time factor, right? Or maybe more a timing factor, when you make your turn and go for it. But what if you don't get that right? What happens then? What did the diagram on his fridge say about that? Not a thing. Not a Goddamn fucking thing.

And when he tries to swim, how far will he get before his heart gives out? Or the Pearlman Shake hits?

Rise and sink. Gulp and spit. That feeling of being heaved into the air, then dropped, arms straight out, fighting for buoyancy and stability. Another large swell upends him, head over heels, and he has to paddle and kick to get upright and breathe. How deep now? And if the tide took J'nelle out, wouldn't she be somewhere nearby fighting to stay alive like he is, somewhere out there in the stormy dark?

A sharp ache gnaws at his ribs, but the water feels different. The sensation of bobbing up and down is now stronger than the outward pull of the sea, the current roils more than it sucks. For a moment, the wind slackens, and he can hear the faraway crash of waves on the beach. Maybe he's out far enough. Maybe this is where he should swim for shore.

He executes a hard scissor kick to turn himself and begins to thrash his way westward down the beach. The distance to shore will be shorter and there will be less chance of drifting out to sea. He takes in a mouthful of water with every stroke, has to stop and tread water for a moment to vomit, then kicks himself back into motion and on course. And that is when the cramp hits. His left calf muscle jack-knifes upward against his hamstring, and both muscles lock in an ache that torques his entire body.

Jesus, this thing that's got him. This Goddamn Pearlman thing. Is his body in that big a hurry to kill him?

He felt that kind of helplessness once in Vietnam when he was on patrol with the marines near Khe Sanh, packing the PRC-10 radio—a twenty-five pound box of hard plastic and steel they called the "Prick-ten"—to relieve his radioman, and a cramp hit. He fell on his hands and knees in a jungle mountain stream, the muscles in his leg tight as a jeep spring. The marine grunts in file behind him slogged right on by and started up the far bank that went straight up toward the sky and was choked in ten-foot elephant grass. The last man to pass was the marine gunny sergeant.

"Hurt, lieutenant?"

"Cramp."

The gunny reached down, grabbed him by the radio's shoulder straps, and jerked him to his feet.

"Walk it out. Pretend you're a marine."

He pushed Ace to the bank, where the cramp hit even harder, and Ace dropped to all fours. The gunny grabbed him again, this time by his web utility belt, and up the bank they went, scrambling together, dragging Ace's jack-knifed leg. The gunny held his M-14 in one hand and yanked Ace by his middle while Ace grabbed at stalks of elephant grass to pull himself along. When they reached the top, the gunny got him to his feet and gave him a pat on the ass.

"See, lieutenant? Easy as fucking a bowlegged mule."

Now, riding a huge swell, he treads water and massages his calf to loosen the cramp. Down he goes, digging at himself, as the pain screams into the muffled roar of sea. He fights his way back to the surface and digs some more. Finally a slight easing. He kicks, twists his body, and struggles to tread water. The cramp eases some more, then signals a threat to return. The cold water doesn't help, but at least there's no weight on the leg. He keeps at it, rolling about, spitting out water as fast as it comes in. At last the cramp relaxes enough that he can make the leg work again—at least so it's not a hindrance.

Rolling waves start to hoist him higher. The power of the sea now seems to come from behind him, from out there in the limitless darkness. He allows himself a tiny hope of salvation; the waves are rising to make their rush to shore, a huge wind-up of energy to catapult him in.

He stops fighting and tries to ride the swell he is on, adopting it as his ticket home—if he can just hang on, stay slightly in front of it. When he feels it begin to crest, he executes a one-legged scissors kick and swims as hard as he can down the wave's face as it curls tighter and tighter, folding him into its barrel until swimming becomes useless. He is in the air a split second, then flipped over and over and thinks, *This is how I will die— not by drowning but by being beaten to death*. He has an image of his limp and lifeless body, rolling in the surf, up and down the beach, and then all thought is lost in a mad whirling and tumbling until he feels the first scrape of his naked butt against the bottom. Then another flip, and his face grinds into it as well.

He fights to get to his feet, then falls backward in the outrush of the wave that brought him in. Then up again and knocked forward onto his hands and knees by the next incoming wave. He crawls, splashes, and claws his way forward until the retreating water washes past him and he is able to once again get himself upright and onto the soggy beach.

A peppery rain has begun to fall. He staggers forward, collapses at the base of a dune, and gags into the sand. His chest is heaving. A tremor, not from any ailment this time but from pure adrenaline, runs like a current from his chin to the tips of his toes. His arms, braced on the sand and bent like spider legs, begin to shake. His left hamstring and calf muscle twitch and threaten to jerk themselves back into the cramp.

Jesus, he's lucky he could swim at all.

He glances quickly up and down the beach before his elbows give and he rolls onto his side in the sand in a fetal position, hands clasped between his knees.

"Damn it," he says, spitting bile into the sand. "Where in the name of God is she?"

He sucks in air and calls, "J'nelle, J'nelle." His voice is gargled and croaky and quickly lost in the crash of waves and buzz of the wind about his ears. His butt and elbows are skinned from where he ground into the sand. Water blows from the end of his nose and clings coldly to his skin. He starts to shake. He cannot allow this. *Pretend you're a marine, the gunny said—like Seth, J'nelle's*

147

husband who leaped into the glacier's black oblivion. He massages his leg some more, then pushes himself to his feet and stands spread-legged to keep his balance and rubs his arms and thighs and shanks to stave off the shivers. He has to find her.

He peers more carefully in each direction, up and down the beach. Nothing but darkness and the booming ocean. Lines of foam the color of a fish belly quiver with a vaguely luminescent glow. He has never been on this beach in this kind of weather. It could be a beach in any part of the world.

So, which way? She is a far better swimmer than he, so maybe farther down the beach. Or maybe she was able to fight the tide sooner and came ashore in the other direction. Or maybe… no not that, not that.

He starts down the beach, still headed west, calling with his croaky voice, alternately rubbing and hugging himself, sucking and blowing air. After a few yards, he stops. Why west? They entered the water farther east, and when they came out for their get-together stroll on Friday and she had her Mason Morrel confession moment, they had walked even farther eastward. He turns and picks up his pace, trying to make his voice work, calling into the wind like the squeak of a small animal. He is almost running now, forcing his calf and hamstring to stretch through the remnant ache of the cramp. The tightness in his chest is back. His heart pounds in his ears above the thud of the waves.

He has gone a hundred feet past the place where they went into the water when he sees her figure against the backdrop of the dunes. She is on her knees, sitting back on her heels with her head bowed, gripping her thighs. He croaks a yell, but she does not hear him, and he is almost to her before she looks up.

"Oh, Ace!"

She leaps up, throws herself against him, and holds him to her, digging her fingers into his back. It is like being grabbed by something feral, and it comes to him in a fuzzy sort of way that she is naked, that they are both naked, out here on this beach in the wind and rain of a gathering storm. He remembers a picture of Adam and Eve in the Bible his parents gave him as a kid, copied from a famous painter who portrayed the first two humans on earth, slinking away through a jungle darkened by the wrath of God. Against the angry sky and green-black foliage, Eve's pale Renaissance body shown luminously white and beckoned Ace to join their flight. And suddenly in this moment, here with J'nelle, he feels he is finally out of that dark garden. He clings to her and they cling to each other as the night roils around them.

Her face is slick with rain and tears, and she is shaking. Her wet hair clings to her skull and neck and makes her seem rinsed down into yet another version of herself, and he feels he is holding the truth of this new, older J'nelle for the first time.

"Oh, God," she says. "Oh, Ace."

He catches his breath for what feels like the first time since they waded into the water.

"It's OK," he says. "It's OK."

They hold on to each other a moment longer before their grips loosen.

"I looked all over," she says.

"You swam east?"

"No, I just came out of the wave near where we dove in and you were gone. I've been frantic. I thought you'd hurt yourself somehow and couldn't swim."

"Rip current," he says.

She hugs him again, keeps saying she is sorry for suggesting the swim in the first place, for leading him into it. She calls herself an idiot, a fool. It is the same voice he heard that morning when she blamed herself for failing to help Seth.

Ace starts to shiver. She rubs her hands briskly up and down his back and ribs, then squeezes him close again. They hold the embrace, then turn, hand in hand, and start down the beach to the path through the dunes to the house. The rain comes harder.

On the path, Ace retrieves their beach towels and clothing and holds her towel like a cloak for her to step into. "It's wet," he says, as he wraps it around her shoulders that seem thin under the weight of the towel. He gathers the sweatshirt and underwear and takes her hand. They start toward the house.

The tremor hits stronger than any he has felt. It yanks at his shoulder and runs through his biceps to his forearm, then torques the wrist of the hand she is holding. The hand itself starts to crimp. She tightens her grip, then steps quickly ahead of him, turns on tiptoe, and pulls him close. The kiss is open, insistent. It melts him completely. They go down together as she throws the beach towel out beneath her on the sand. He tries to brace himself and mumbles something about going back to the house, but it is muffled in the greedy opening and pressing of lips as she pulls him down on top of her. He tries again to brace himself, but the tremor returns, and he collapses completely onto his elbows that are planted on either side of her shoulders.

Beneath him her hips and rear end are pressed hard into the sand, but her movement does not stop, just as it did not when they tried it in high school on the grave. And he thinks he will fail once again, for the second time this night, and not because he does not have a condom or because he is an old man, but because he will just fail. She clasps him tight. Her thin, precise fingers find his penis and stroke it and stroke it as she guides him in. It is like being on the ocean again, with its own feeling of drowning, except the undulation is soft and smooth like the slow wash of waves, and the few shuddering seconds it takes for him to finish seem to last for hours.

His hope, his determination, to hold on for her to finish is the dream of a younger man.

After it is over, he lies beside her and lets the rain wash his face. Even in the watery, wind-whipped night, the smell of their just finished sex rises off them and clings in the air, while the storm, the night, and the ocean rage far away in the darkness beyond the dunes.

They rise slowly and walk back to the house, carrying the beach towels, now doubly heavy with both rainwater and sand. She suggests he go to an emergency room so someone can check him over, just to be safe. "Too far away," he says. "I'm OK."

"Stubborn," she says.

When they step into the house, he takes her hand.

"I'm sorry," he says, "that it happened so fast. I mean, that I couldn't hold on. It's been awhile."

She goes to tiptoe and gives him a quick peck. "Don't worry," she says, "these days, it takes a while."

She folds her arms and gives him a curious, questioning look.

"You know," she says, "that this has gotten completely out of hand."

"Yeah," he says, "I know. And it started to do that when you walked in the door in what seems like at least a week ago."

Before he can make it to the shower, a chill hits. He stumbles into the shower stall and holds to the grab bar until the hot water warms him up enough to stand on his own. He dries himself quickly, finds some iodine for his scrapes, and puts on his clothes. Another tremor threatens to hit; he cannot be sure if it is the Pearlman Shake or the beginning of another chill. He finds a moth-eaten quilt in the back of a closet, wraps it about himself, and goes to the liquor cabinet over the sink.

She glides toward him across the great room floor in a lightweight robe, takes the offered glass of brandy, rests back against the counter, and begins to sip. Her hair is fluffed but still wet and hangs to her shoulders in a springy mass that somehow makes her features even sharper, her eyes brighter, those twitches in her lips even more subtle and quick.

"Your hair looks good," he says.

"I've already said 'F you' once today."

"No, really," he says, "it looks great both dry and wet."

She glances up at him, the brandy glass halfway to her lips. "What did we learn from this?" she says.

He gives her a puzzled look.

"I mean the ocean thing," she says. "The midnight swim."

"I don't know," he says. "What did you learn?"

"That the impulsive demon that has screwed up my life is still here."

She takes a large sip of brandy.

Midnight J'nelle, he thinks. There was no reason to anticipate that, after high school, that side of her would simply vanish. He tries to imagine her in college after she left him, pregnant and scared, setting up her abortion, probably from a payphone somewhere off campus.

"I went willingly," he says. "Once we got started, I wanted to do it as much as you did."

She rubs the wet rim of her glass over her lips, stares once again at the floor, and sighs.

"Ace, I'm totally at sea here, no pun intended. I mean really disoriented in so many ways. I need to pull back a bit and catch my breath." She draws a long intake of air and lets it out slowly. "I guess what I'm saying is, I need to go to bed and think."

She takes another sip, lowering her mouth to the

153

glass rather than raising the glass to her lips. He thinks again of a bird drinking water.

"Or maybe best to not think," she says. Her eyes stay on him as she drinks the last of her brandy.

A tiredness descends that seeps through to his bones. "It wouldn't hurt me to be alone awhile myself."

"Thanks," she says. "I'd give you a goodnight peck like last night, but given our recent history, I'm afraid I'll start something. So I'll just say goodnight."

He raises his glass to her with a slight wobble. "Goodnight."

He watches her fade into the shadowy hallway. When her door shuts, he turns the TV on to the weather channel. Category 3, dead on course, could build to Category 4 or 5 before it makes landfall after midnight tomorrow.

Shit.

He sinks into the couch, bathed in the flickering light from the TV. He could fall asleep right here—it's a long walk, at least forty feet to his bedroom. His mind fades in and out, mumbling to itself. He could have died out there. And yes, he was scared—he might as well admit it—but it was not of death so much, it was of defeat, an end to that desperate illusion that he could escape a reckoning with the great unknown.

Around him, windows rattle. Gusts of wind whistle about the eaves, throw rain onto the porch roof, and send it tapping against the side of the house. From above, there is a thud and scrape as one of the hammock chairs, blown over by the wind, skitters across the deck floor. This is not a groaning house, but he fancies it groans at him all the same.

It will get worse all through the day tomorrow.

And what will he do—just shut the place up and drive away, leave it to its fate, a hundred-year-old family home? If the house goes, what will become of the family ghosts? *You owe us*, they might say. *The house was left to you. You owe it to everyone to take care of it.* They are probably hovering about right now, watching him. But the ancient ones, out there in the thicket guarding their graves, maybe they'll be glad to see the house go. Maybe glad to see him go as well.

The ocean will claim even their land someday, and we will all be ancient ones.

But not yet. He is still here. He proved that tonight when he fought his way out of that ocean.

And so what is his duty, his obligation? And to whom? Himself, the ghosts, the house itself?

After the storm there could be looting, just like Faye-Marie said. Island druggies—friends of the young mother he surrendered his water to in the supermarket—waiting for a chance to rush in and take whatever they can carry off and sell for a bag, a bottle of pills, a needle, a hit. In the closet of his bedroom, there's a twelve-gauge pump shotgun left by his father. Ace used it a couple of years ago to shoot down a drone some asshole kept flying over his house. Bam! right off the upper deck. The guy who owned it came to Ace's house in a rage. "Sue me," Ace said. He has no idea where the shells for the gun are now, and he probably wouldn't have the nerve to use it against anyone if he did.

Pam would have approved of that shot off the deck, even admired his aim. She might have shot the drone herself; she was as good a shot as he is.

And J'nelle? That impulsive demon in her might applaud, but the former high school scholar and class president? He's not so sure she exists anymore.

But this thing that's happening between them, whatever it is, *does* exist. And what is he going to do about it—pack up and leave, follow her off the island and on to the Raleigh airport, walk with her to the security checkpoint, say goodbye and watch as she passes through the X-ray machine and walks off into her old life of schedules and daily routines and a pending medical report and leaves him flopping like a fish on the creaky deck of his life? And then what? Back to occasional emails, so that the last two days will have been just an old-timers' weekend fling, albeit a fling he managed to consummate against all the odds.

Albeit on the second try.

He at least has that to be proud of—just a little. And for a moment, as they lay together out there among the rain-drenched dunes, it felt like he had finally caught up with her.

He heaves a great sigh and inhales deeply in what feels like a grab for the oxygen he was unable to get earlier when he pulled himself from the sea, then feels about on the couch next to him for the remote and switches to the sports channel to check on the Sox. Another win, 14 to 2. Amazing—anything can happen.

He wakes before dawn, still seated on the couch, neck and back bent and aching, deep in his calf muscle a wedge of pain where the cramp hit. The events of the night before seem hazy, yet intimate and close, like a new companion whose features have not quite formed. He brushes his hand across the couch seat next to him, then looks about in the semidarkness. The room feels unusually large and empty. The wind thumps at the side of the house, less agitated than last night but heavier, stronger.

He goes to his bathroom to shave, then returns to the main room and sits in the recliner in the early light to read the Sunday *Times* on his iPad between bouts of nodding off. He should have gotten his ass off the couch last night and gone to bed. He has a feeling she did not sleep well either, a feeling based on nothing except, well, a feeling.

The wind comes harder against the house. He ought to turn on the TV and check on the storm.

The sound of her bedroom door opening and closing brings him fully awake for the first time.

"Good morning," he says.

"Good morning."

She has on the same lightweight robe she wore the night before. There is something sleepy and dreamlike about the flow of it as she moves on bare feet across the hardwood floor in the light from his reading lamp and the yellow-gray dawn. She has brought the shape back to her hair—he thought he heard the hair dryer—but its former sheen is gone, washed away, he assumes, by the brine of the ocean during their midnight swim, its red-gold tint faded to rust smeared with gray. No make-up, no perfume. The wrinkles at the corners of her eyes and lips are more visible—tiny trenches dug by time—and the lips themselves are more relaxed.

"Sorry," he says. "I haven't made coffee."

"Instant is fine with me," she says.

"In the cupboard next to the sink."

She dumps a double dose into a mug, adds tap water, and places it in the microwave. Then does the same for him.

"What's happening with the storm?" she says.

"I was just about to check."

They stand together before the TV and watch the hyperactive weathercasters say the same thing over and over in different ways: still a big storm, still coming, landfall just after midnight.

"Right on target," he says.

She blows steam from her coffee and takes a sip. "So?"

"So what?"

"What can I do to help you close things up and get out of here?"

"Your flight's at 2:30?"

She nods.

"You ought to leave by 8:30 just to be sure. The roads may be crowded."

"That gives us over two hours. What can I do to help?"

"Right now, you can relax and drink your coffee. I'll make us some breakfast. Then we can plan our escape."

She props herself on a high stool to drink her coffee while he breaks eggs into a poacher to start breakfast. Her features have an overcast look, and her pale blue-green eyes, that he used to feel shine out at him even in the darkness, are now focused inward.

"It'll be OK," he says. "It's a simple house. Doesn't take much time to close things up. If we get in a crunch, you can go ahead, and I'll come later."

She sets down the coffee. "You're not planning to leave, are you?"

"Why do you say that?"

"Just a hunch."

"I guess maybe I'm not."

"Why?"

"The house. I sorta feel I should stick with it as long as I can."

"That doesn't seem very wise."

"Maybe this time, wisdom is not the wisest thing."

"Does it also have something to do with those medical tests waiting for you when you get home?"

"Possibly."

"And maybe what happened between us last night?"

159

"Maybe. And please don't ask me how that computes. I have no idea."

She picks up her coffee to take a sip, but sets it down and says in a whisper, "I didn't sleep much last night."

"Me either."

"I'm afraid to even begin to talk about why."

"Me too."

"So maybe we should just leave it for now."

"Yeah."

He empties the eggs onto plates and adds toast. They take their seats at the table and eat in a silence that feels buffeted by the storm. Petals of various colors from the flowers he bought two days before have shed and fallen onto the table. In his haste on Friday, he forgot to fill the vase with water.

She speaks in a forced way as if what she says is memorized: "Ace, I need to say again how sorry I am I coaxed you into last night's swim. It was inexcusable."

"I'm not sorry," he says.

She picks up a flower petal. It is violet around the edges, white in the middle. She studies it a moment, and looks at him.

"Sometimes," she says, "the petals are prettier after they shed."

"Yeah," he says, "just before they fade."

After they eat, he cleans the kitchen while she dresses and packs. Then he goes out to the front porch and roof deck to pull in furniture and close the window shutters, which is a struggle because the latches are caked with generations of paint. The wind picks up steadily, whips the tops of beach pines, bends the limbs of the live oaks, and drives light rain against the house. When the wind gusts, the rain is horizontal, and by the time Ace has finished with the shutters, the bottom half of him below his rain jacket is soaked.

He enters through the back door, takes a towel from the linen closet to dry himself, and finds her in the main room with her back to him, putting up dishes and glasses from the drying rack and dishwasher, clad once again in her jeans and last night's turtleneck. She has turned on all the lights, and with the shutters closed, the room has taken on a stormy, yellow-green hue.

He comes to stand beside her and rest his hands on the edge of the counter.

"I haven't seen this domestic side of you," he says.

"This is about as far as it goes."

"Don't worry about it. I can finish it after you've gone. Let's talk."

She turns, leans back against the counter with her arms crossed, and sighs.

"OK," she says, "you first."

He turns the same way she is facing and stares out into the room.

"Nothing has felt that good in a long time."

"You almost drowned."

"Nah. I had it licked from the get-go."

"It didn't seem quite that way to me."

"Sure I did. But I think you know that's really not the part I'm talking about."

"Yes, I know," she says, "but in my case there's that

similar feeling of—how does Bonnie Raitt say it in her song, 'Something to Talk About'?—'going under.'"

"And that scares you?"

"Yes."

A tremble runs down his left forearm. He tightens his grip on the counter and slowly releases it.

"I'm not leaving either," she says. "If that's OK."

All those things he used to do as a lawyer: rush in, reason, talk sense; all those persuasive skills he honed over the years, still there somewhere, rusty but ready to use.

"Is it OK?" she says.

"No, but…"

"But what?"

"Please stay anyway."

She moves close, circles her arm under his and takes his hand.

"I'll cancel my flight," she says. "But before I do, I assume you have a plan where we won't get killed."

"Yes, but it just got more complicated."

"We have food?"

"Yes."

"Water?"

"Yes."

"More candles?"

"Yes, plus a lantern and a small generator that runs the well pump and fridge."

"It doesn't sound that complicated."

"Ever been in a hurricane?" he says.

"No."

"I have, a small one. The one headed our way is not small, and if it gets as bad as they say it might, it could blow this old house away."

She moves closer and rests her cheek against his shoulder. He ignores another twitch in his hand and tightens his grip on hers. "Still sure you want to stay?"

"Isn't there a local shelter?"

"Usually the high school gymnasium," he says. "But there is also a shelter here, out back."

"A storm shelter? I hadn't noticed it."

"It's easy to miss," he says, "part of the landscape next to the woods. Actually it's a bomb shelter built during the Cold War by my uncle Hobart Sinclair who was convinced the Russians had it in for him personally because he owned a Chrysler dealership and Chrysler made American tanks. So naturally he was at the top of Stalin's hit list. He built a shelter at his home in Columbia and one here for when he was on vacation."

"So if it gets bad, we can go there."

"Maybe. I haven't looked inside it in years."

"Let's look," she says, "and the answer is, yes, I want to stay."

The shelter is a bunker of reinforced concrete, banked on three sides with dirt and sand. The front of it is protected by a second concrete wall spaced two feet from the bunker and joined to it on one side by a connecting wall. A rusty tin roof runs from the top of the protecting wall to the front wall of the bunker, so that to enter, you have to duck under the roof to open the bunker's steel door. Two sheltered air vents with small fans, set at ground level, ensure ventilation—as long as the electricity works.

Ace uses a crowbar to pry the rusty door open, and the two of them step inside. A cold-crypt smell greets them. A hard layer of dust that has settled during the passing years, covers everything: walls, floor, the bare lightbulb hanging from the ceiling, and four canvas army cots, folded and stacked against each other in a corner. Against the back wall is a stand of shelves, empty except for a few mason jars and two rusty cans of Del Monte peaches. Next to the shelves is a small table.

"Needs a woman's touch," Ace says.

"F you number three," she says.

"I'm halfway serious."

"OK, Mr. Clean, let's get to work."

They sweep, dust, scrape mold, and sweep some more, beat out two of the canvas folding cots and cover them with comforters to serve as mattresses. They bring in a chain saw and an old Coleman stove, then return to the house to cook fish, eggs, bacon, and other perishables from the refrigerator, pack them in a large cooler with ice and Freez Paks, and roll the cooler to the shelter. They haul out coffee and other staples, water, candles, pillows, and two comforters. Ace runs an extension cord from the generator to feed the shelter's one light bulb, and after an extended search, finds the shells to the shotgun. Over J'nelle's objection—"I never imagined you'd be a gun nut"—he adds the gun to the survival stockpile. The rain comes and goes, but the wind does not stop and blows in gusts so strong that occasionally they have to set down what they are carrying and grab onto each other to keep their balance. Through it all, his tremors start, stop, and start again. The closer the storm feels, the more they seem to want to take hold.

Sunday evening

Around nightfall, as his last acts of preparation, Ace moves his car out to the main road and parks it, then parks J'nelle's in an open area as far from the house and trees as possible.

They return to the main room of the house and turn on the weather channel while they prepare supper. Weather newscasters pass the broadcast in breathless frenzy from the smartly dressed duo in the TV studio to others on the coast in flapping rain gear, leaning into the wind to keep their balance. A young woman reporter hunkers, like a dough boy in a foxhole, behind a grass-covered dune a mile down the beach from Ace's house. She clutches at the hood of her L.L. Bean storm jacket and shouts over wind static to explain how tide movement will affect wave height and storm surge. "Let's take a look," she says, and stretches her neck to peek over the dune toward the beach where the waves smack like cannon shot and hurl strings of slobber-like spray. She turns and slides back down the dune to safety.

"Well, you can see what we are facing. And that surf will be twice to three times as high by two a.m. We are in for a long night. Back to you, Leslie."

Leslie, in her bright red dress and winged black hair, grabs the baton and runs with it: Freya's intensity will increase over the warm water near shore and probably hit as at least a Category 4. The station cuts to the governor, surrounded by law enforcement officers and emergency responders, as he issues dire warnings. The officers and responders step forward one at a time to drive the warnings home and speak personally to the laggards who have failed to heed the evacuation order: stay away from the beach, do not try to drive, seek refuge at shelters such as schools and churches.

"You know," Ace says, "our cell phones aren't going to work in that bunker. We could still leave. They haven't closed Highway 16."

"We could," she says.

They sit down to baked red snapper, spinach sautéed in olive oil, garlic, pine nuts and feta, and a bottle of not-bad Malbec from the island grocery. The news continues on the TV, switching back and forth from regular coverage to the storm, and then entirely to the storm. J'nelle asks hesitant, half-stated questions about what it was like the night before when Ace was caught in the riptide, his feelings, his fears, how he managed his escape. He answers like a junior high student, caught in questions on a book he did not understand. "I don't know," he says, "I don't know." And then suddenly he hears himself say:

"It was all mixed up, swirling around me in the storm—images of people, voices, you and Pam, my kids and grandkids, friends. You were all there, and then, one by one the images faded, all except you and Pam. Or maybe it was more like I faded from them."

He feels her gaze on him as he slowly shakes his head.

"The two of you stayed very close by, and I shouldn't say this, but you seemed to distill into one being that spoke with two voices. You were calling on me to live; she was giving me the strength to die."

He pauses and looks at her, caught in the puzzlement of what he has just said.

"I'm sorry," he says. "I didn't mean to compare you to Pam. I just…"

He feels his face widen in desperation.

"That's it, though, isn't it?" he says. "That's where I'm stuck in my ripening old age: between the yearn to live and the need for courage to die."

"Most of us are," she says, "but it's not either/or."

"It can be a lonely place," he says.

"Yes."

He goes to the sink and pours out the last of his wine. In the window over the sink, he can see the reflection of her sitting at the table in the glow of a single candle left over from the night before. She is in another variation of that prayerful pose, her fingers splayed at the base of her wine glass, turning it gently on the table surface.

"Maybe by morning," he says, "the storm will have made the whole thing moot. But meanwhile, let's make a run for the bunker."

Sunday night

They arrange the two cots perpendicular to the front wall of the bunker and sit on the cots facing each other. Her hands are pressed between her knees. She glances about the small space, cramped with the two open cots and two folded ones and the provisions they have brought from the house. Through the thick steel door, the sounds of the storm are muted. But it is still out there like an animal on the prowl, growling, circling.

"Why four cots?" she says. "There isn't space for more than two when they are open."

"Sometimes," he says, "Uncle Hobart didn't think things through so well. He had, as they say, an alcohol problem."

Ace is hunched over, gripping the edge of the cot he's seated on. "Truth is, he was a four-flushing drunk."

"Are you OK?" she says.

"No. I can't do this, sit here in this tight space. It's like the bunkers we got shelled in in Vietnam. And these military style cots don't help."

"Back to the house?" she says.

"No."

He puts on his rain gear with trembling fingers, adjusts the hood, and uses his foot to shove the metal door

169

open a hand's width. Rain drops spatter in. Outside, wind whistles, trees groan, limbs pop and break, unknown objects skitter and strike other objects. The ocean roars above the shriek of the storm.

Ace takes a seat on the concrete floor next to the door and faces out into the air lock between the bunker and front wall, with his arms draped over his knees. The tin roof shields him from the worst of the rain, but the wind whips through and blows out the candles. If the generator goes, they will be completely in the dark.

"Do you want to talk some more about Vietnam?" she says.

"No."

He can feel her there behind him, not moving, her eyes on the back of his head.

"I'm sorry," he says.

"It's OK. I just want to help."

"Do you want to talk some more about Seth and your daughter?"

"There's not much else to say."

"He sounds like a brave man."

"Yes, he was very brave."

The space between them fills with an empty silence.

"I slapped Anna once," she says, "really hard. She was only fifteen and small for her age, and I didn't know how strong I was. I'd been playing a lot of tennis, in sort of a compulsive way to take out my anger over her behavior and Seth's increasing non-involvement with everything. She came in late one night drunk, probably on drugs as well, a good two hours past her curfew.

170

She'd been pulling this sort of thing for months, and finally I'd had it. We got into a nasty argument. She had her share of teenage surliness, but I'd never seen her like that, fists at her side, hurling curses. At one point I thought she was going to spit. The slap was reflexive, like my whole body convulsed. I hit her so hard she fell backwards against a chair and then down on her knees. I stood over her daring her to get up. She kept her head down until I finally backed a few steps away. I continued to look down at her bowed head, and I remembered how it felt against my chest when she was a baby and Seth and I cuddled her for the first time at the adoption center. She was so tiny. Her eyes were closed, and on her squinched little face was the most heartbreaking mixture of obliviousness and hope. And her hands—baby hands with that look of not being quite formed, fingers crimped yet moving as if to grab onto something.

"I looked down at the hand I'd slapped her with. The hot sting in it radiated all over me. My muscles were tense, my wrist primed and ready to strike again. I began to shake all over. She started to get up, and I reached out to her, but she pulled away. My handprint glowed bright red on her pale face, so different from my complexion and Seth's. There were tears in her eyes, but she would not let them spill. Her jaws were clinched, and she had that stomach-turning look of both the deepest kind of hurt and the hottest kind of hatred.

"She started toward the front door. I lunged and grabbed her arm, but she jerked it away, ran out the door, and slammed it behind her, right in my face.

I threw it open and watched her as she ran down the street in front of our condo, down the middle of it, and out of sight. It was the first time she ran away. I finally found her living with a family in a rough part of town. I think the parents were using drugs. She was out of school and therefore away from friends she was close to, and she clearly was not getting enough to eat. I talked her into coming home. But it was never the same; it only got worse."

He is about to say that being a parent is hard and that what she did is understandable, that he might have reacted similarly if his kids had gone on drugs and cursed him and Pam. Instead he says: "And you are not able to forgive yourself."

"No. Every time I try, I hear that slap. I see her face as a baby when I lifted her from the crib at the adoption center. Except her baby eyes are wide open, staring at me."

"I'm sorry, J'nelle."

"Thanks," she says, "me too."

Ace listens as the storm lashes the nearby trees and the metal roof over the cubby between the protective wall and front door of the bunker. Rain through the crack in the door pops on the hood of his rain jacket and drips into a puddle forming around him on the floor. If he could bear to move away from the open door and back into the bunker, he would get up, sit next to her on the cot and hold her. Instead he reaches behind him and touches her ankle and squeezes it, then slowly lets it go and leans forward again, arms crooked over his knees.

"I had a case once," he says, "that haunts me, especially late at night when I wake up and realize I'm alone. In the late 1980s, I represented a guy in Paxton County, up near the Virginia border, for assaulting his wife. He beat her so bad she spent two days in the hospital. This guy was a real piece of work: rich, arrogant mama's boy without an ounce of pity or remorse. The criminal defense bar in Paxton County didn't want anything to do with him, so his parents came all the way to Raleigh to hire me. I was working hard to build a reputation then and took the case. Plus, I believed and still do, that even an asshole like him deserves a fair trial."

How long has it been, Ace thinks, since he heard himself say something as lofty as that?

"The victim, the young wife, was the opposite of my client: nice, pretty, and from a decidedly un-wealthy family. I couldn't imagine why she married him until I met her mother, a pushy social climber who had bullied her daughter into trying to fulfill her own dreams of being haughty and rich.

"The first DA assigned to the case was a woman I knew in law school named LuAnne Butterfield. LuAnne was sharp, refused right off to negotiate a plea to a lesser charge. So I knew from the start the case had to be tried. And of course the problem was I had no defense. My client was twice the size of his wife, and he beat the hell out of her."

Ace pauses. "J'nelle, tell me if you don't want to hear any more of this. It's not a very heartwarming story."

"Go on," she says. "I'm listening."

173

"My client kept saying his wife was cheating on him. I didn't believe him. She looked like the last person in the world who'd cheat on her husband. And what if she did? It was no excuse for the assault. But his family had money, so we hired an investigator. And to my amazement, it turned out she was having an affair and had been for over a year, with a married man.

"So there I was. Obnoxious client. No plea to a lesser offense possible. Horrible facts. And no defense. But Paxton County was a hotbed of Bible thumpers who weren't going to like adultery. At the trial, I played the only card I had. I went after the wife about her affair. And I was lucky. By then, LuAnne had left the DA's office, and they'd run in a second stringer named Wilmer Warlick, a good ole boy who didn't care a damn about women's rights. And Wilmer was a drinker. I saw him a couple of times nodding off at the counsel table. He put up the victim's testimony in a half-assed way, no medical evidence, and rested his case. On cross examination, I started right in on her about the affair. Wilmer sat and picked his nose and shuffled papers.

"As I hoped, she denied the affair. Of course Wilmer hadn't spent a minute preparing her, and he sat there while I hit her with the details, one-by-one, like Chinese water torture. She alternated between looking down at her hands knotted in her lap, and then up at her mother in the audience, who was giving her a look that dripped with anger. As tensely as those hands were knotted, I could see her arms shaking. But I was into it by then, doing my best work. When I sensed she was on the verge of tears, I stopped, thanked her very politely for her testimony, and let her go. Wilmer offered no redirect, just sat there like a frog in the road."

Ace pauses. The noise of the storm seems far away. The overhead light bulb sways slightly on its cord and casts his hooded shadow on the inside of the bunker door.

"After that, it was easy. I called her boyfriend to impeach her testimony. He was almost as big a prick as my client, fancy dresser, slicked back hair, and dumb. By the time I was done with him, he'd blabbed everything, almost bragged about it. So there was Wilmer with his only witness exposed for all to see as a liar. The case could have gone to the jury, an all-white, mostly male group of hard-shell Baptists if I ever saw one, but the judge, who by then was thoroughly disgusted with Wilmer, took pity on the young wife and dismissed it."

Ace pauses again. The shadow on the door sits there like a third person, listening, waiting. He draws a deep breath.

"I jammed an elbow into my client, and we left. I avoided looking at the wife on the way out, as she sat with her parents on the front row behind the counsel table. But with every step I took up that aisle, I left a bit of myself behind. My client shook my hand when we were outside in the hallway and gave his head an arrogant jerk I'd come to detest, throwing a curl of drooping bangs off his forehead. His mother beamed. His daddy clapped me on the back—hard—over and over, which gave me a hint of where his son's violent nature might have come from.

"I drove back to my office in Raleigh, put away the file, and went back to what I thought of as my normal life. Three months later, my client killed her. He didn't rely on his fists that time; he used a brass-handled poker. The officers who arrested him said her face was unrecognizable. They made a point of driving all the way from Paxtonville to the Raleigh courthouse to show me the pictures of her corpse and stood there waiting to hear what I had to say. Which was, of course, nothing."

Ace draws another long breath that seems to levitate him in the thick air of the shelter.

"His parents tried to hire me to handle his murder case. No way. I forget who represented him, but he received a life sentence. Probably out by now. I've tried to hear as little as possible about him. But I cannot forget the utter defeat and shame on that young woman's face when I had her on the stand. Everything she had tried to make of herself, every desperate hope for salvaging her life, everything she had tried to hold onto was destroyed. And I cannot forget the look in my client's eyes as we stood with his parents in the hallway after the case's dismissal. It was a look of glee, but there was something in it that was deadly, as if what he had done was condoned by the ease with which I destroyed her case and justified by the judge's ruling. I had abused her myself, I'd joined in on the mayhem, so it was alright; it was legal. And when I think back on that moment, I knew even then: the beatings would go on, and sooner or later, one would very likely be fatal."

Ace cups his palm, holds it to the crack in the steel door, and rubs the collected rainwater over his face.

"That's the hardest story of my life," he says, "worse than Vietnam, because I did everything I thought I was supposed to do. I exceeded myself, put every skill I had to work for my client, I followed every ethical rule. I took a case that other lawyers wouldn't touch, and I won. But, the price! That case called into question my view of who I was; it challenged the myth of my moral self-esteem; it tore down the self-righteous scaffolding upon which I'd built my career."

He pauses. "Upon which I'd built my life."

His mind is emptied of words. His head seems to bow itself. He shakes it slowly back and forth.

She lowers herself from the cot onto the floor beside him, puts her arm around his shoulder, and holds him close.

The numbness in his mind stays until a shudder in his shoulders shakes it loose. He's sure she feels it.

"I'm sitting in a big puddle," he says. "You're gonna get wet."

"Yes," she says, "I probably will."

Somewhere in the distance, through the storm, a siren sounds. The lightbulb flickers as the electricity goes out and the generator kicks in.

"How long will that run?" she says.

"Until it runs out of gas or a limb crashes through the shed it's in and crushes it."

"Let's turn it off now," she says, "the light. Maybe it will help with your claustrophobia. There's freedom in darkness."

"It certainly turned out that way last night," he says.

"And what if we move your cot closer to the door opening so you can lie with your head in the fresh air coming in through the crack—will that help?"

"Maybe—we can try."

She gets to her feet and pushes his cot near the door, then switches off the light. Ace stretches out on the cot with his head as near the door opening as he can get it. The cot's damp canvas gives off a moldy odor that reminds him of Vietnam. The comforters and pillow from the house are swollen with moisture. He wraps a blanket around him and breathes slowly, sucking in the air from the storm.

She speaks from her cot on the other side of the bunker.

"I feel like I'm in a dark corner a million miles away."

"We can move your cot this way," he says, "but you'll get even wetter than you are."

"I'm willing to take my chances, and if I'm going to get wet anyway, I may as well have it all."

She throws off her blanket and moves to join him on his cot.

"Not sure this will hold us both," he says.

"If it breaks, we've got three more."

"I don't think I can offer a repeat of last night," he says.

"Just hold me," she says, "and stop worrying about what you can and can't do."

They lie together as they did the night before, his arm over her, holding the blanket around them while the storm rages. Her body feels steamy to him under her clothes. Ace strains to hear the boom of the ocean over the howling wind. The waves, he thinks—the waves must be over the dunes and into the yard. Near the bunker, one of the live oaks splits and whumps the ground. Its branches crash against the top of bunker.

She flinches, scrunches closer against him.

"It's as bad as they predicted," he says.

"This shelter seems a shrunken place," she says, "and everything out there so far away: cities, highways, airlines, schedules, medical tests, laptops. It's hard to believe it ever existed."

"It's there," he says, "and it'll be there in the morning."

She sighs and shrinks her body even closer to him. Under her ribs he can feel her heartbeat gradually slow its pace.

"I hope you know," he says, "that I didn't plan to seduce you when I invited you down."

"You didn't seduce me."

"Are you sure about that?"

"Yes."

"Did you plan to seduce me?"

"I don't think so. But anyway I didn't seduce you either."

"So, what? We seduced each other?"

She does not answer.

"We each seduced ourselves?" he says.

"Let's not talk anymore," she says. "Let's just be."

Monday morning

After a while, J'nelle moves back to her cot and falls asleep. Ace folds up his wet cot, replaces it with a dry one, and begins to doze in and out. Around two a.m., the wind begins to slacken. A large tree falls somewhere beyond the house, and then things slowly quieten, except for the crash of waves over the dunes.

By dawn, all is eerily quiet. Even the ocean has settled. Its waves wash in and out with a healing sound. Ace takes a deep breath, moves his cot toward the middle of the bunker, and kneels on it to turn on the light bulb without standing on the wet floor. The switch clicks, the light does not come on.

He finds the flashlight, puts his shoulder to the door, and scrapes it open.

"Wait," J'nelle says. "I'm coming."

The dawn has a greenish, splintered hue that is charged with smells of wet sand, blasted wood, and shredded leaves. They step from under the tin roof, still in their rain jackets, and run their eyes quickly over the fallen trunks and crisscrossed limbs toward the house. It has been ripped apart. One half is askew of the other and has slipped from its foundation into the yard. Much of the other half is caved in under a large limb, split from the nearest live oak. What appears to be a second part of that limb, sent flying by the storm, has crashed through the front window and hood of J'nelle's rental car.

"Oh, Ace," she says. "I'm so sorry."

He ducks back under the sheltered front of the bunker, pulls out the chain saw, and goes to work cutting his way through the trunks and limbs toward the house. She follows, helping him pull cut branches out of the way. In an hour, they've cleared a path that lets them through to walk around the house. The front porch roof is off, the upper deck collapsed onto what's left of the porch itself. Most of the shutters are gone or left sagging and the windows are blown out. The dunes have vanished, washed away by the pounding waves and their backwash, leaving a small lake in the front yard.

"For some reason," he says, "losing those dunes feels like the final blow."

They try their cell phones, get no signal, and walk back to sit on a log by the bunker to drink Thermos coffee and eat their breakfast of hard-boiled eggs and cold bacon.

"I wonder how widespread this is," she says.

"All over," he says. "I'll be amazed if the Crowbank Inlet Bridge is standing. We should fire up the chain saw after breakfast and cut our way out to the beach road and see if my car starts. Maybe we can be of some help to people."

They eat in silence broken only by the slow, back-and-forth wash of the sea. J'nelle finally speaks.

"How are you feeling today?"

"How are the shakes, you mean?"

"Yes."

"I haven't noticed them for a while."

"That's good, right?"

"They'll be back."

"When I was doing my aid work with the Peace Corps," she says, "I saw lots of people with symptoms like yours. They turned out to be all sorts of things, some not so disabling."

"That's what my doc says, but I think he's lying."

"I'm not."

"I know you're not."

Before him, the broken house is backlit by the blue ocean and the reflecting glare of the morning sun. If a stranger saw the house, he wouldn't know it from a wrecked juke joint or crossroads store.

"It's almost like a mirage," he says. "It's hard to be sure that what was there before the storm was real. Along comes a big wind and takes out everything except memories, and even those seem buffeted and carried away."

"They are not carried away," she says. "In one form or another, they are right here." She taps her temple to indicate his.

Her gesture points him back in time to the old days when, as a kid, he was here with his parents and sister and uncles and aunts and cousins and his grandmother and what felt like the hovering ghost of his grandfather. Then the times with Pam and his kids and later his grandkids—noisy, chaotic, jubilant days when he and Pam seemed to have dragged the best part of their everyday lives here with them. Then the times alone after Pam died. He sees himself in days past, in the kitchen, preparing his supper to eat alone, then climbing to the upper deck to watch the slow drifting headlights. It seems like months since he did that, with J'nelle no more than a puzzle headed his way.

"Escape," she says. "You said in one of your emails that this house was an 'escape.'"

"It was," he says, "but to get away from the hassles of the real world, not to hang with old ghosts."

"Maybe you see our memories of each other the same way," she says, "as an escape from the real world."

"I guess, maybe. Some of the time—don't you?"

"Yes," she says, "but they are a lot more than that. And this old house was too."

After breakfast, Ace removes the padlock from the door to the collapsed generator shed and attaches it to the bunker door so they can lock it. He refills the chain saw with gas mix and bar oil, and with J'nelle's help, begins to cut their way through the downfall blocking the long, twisted driveway. The beach road runs mostly through savanna protected from the sea by short stretches of maritime forest. But the backwash from the nearby sound has done the damage, ripping out swaths of pavement in both directions down the road from Ace's driveway. What pavement remains is scattered with limbs, debris, and downed utility poles. Ace's car is intact, but one side of it has slid into a water-filled ditch.

"We can try to start it later," Ace says. "Charge our cell phones."

They walk south, toward the most populous part of the island, making their way around utility pole wires and washed out places, a couple of times holding hands and wading up to their knees. To their left, in the maritime forest, treetops are twisted and broken. Pines have been stripped of their needles. To their right, over the sound, helicopters crawl like insects across the pale blue sky. Two of them are updated versions of the Chinooks Ace rode in in Vietnam. A few gulls, returned from inland, swoop over the water nearby, and above the broken treetops down the road, a drone with a TV station emblem rises and begins to circle.

"Eerie," he says.

"Yes," she says, "and lonely."

They help each other through a tangle of limbs and palm branches and over a large chunk of upended asphalt.

"It's like one of those apocalyptic scenes you talked about the other day," he says, "the ones they used to scare us with when we were young, about the aftermath of nuclear war."

"Except," she says, "that the sun is shining and we're alive."

He nods his head toward the road before them. "Yes, but what about down there?"

"The sun will still be shining," she says.

A mile farther on, they approach the wreckage of a cluster of shops and businesses: what was once a surfing store; the remains of a kayak rental place with no kayaks in sight; a miniature golf course and waterslide; and an old, shingle-sided motel. They all sag from their foundations. A few are missing roofs. Behind the first row of them is a wrecked trailer park. Trailers are upside down and piled against each other, roofs caved in, sides ripped off. Only the golf course appears unharmed, but as Ace and J'nelle draw closer, they can see that in places the greens and putting tracks have been stripped of fabric down to the concrete and bare wood.

Three men stand in the road in unzipped rain gear, looking about and talking. Two of them wear law enforcement uniforms, and one of them holds a hand-held radio unit. Nearby, an elderly man and woman poke about the rubble of what was once a tackle shop. Farther up the road, two groups of men in military uniforms, each with a leashed German shepherd, prowl about the wreckage of homes while another team that Ace guesses is a special unit of the National Guard, works at a transformer on a downed utility pole.

Ace and J'nelle make their way around scattered boards and part of a shingle roof to the three men who watch their approach as if the two of them are walking out of a battlefield.

Ace introduces himself and J'nelle to the men who nod politely. The two men in uniform are of medium height. They stand with their legs slightly spread.

The younger of them is fit and muscular and holds a kid-sized orange football he's apparently picked from some of the wreckage. The older one has a watermelon stomach that pokes beyond the opening in his rain gear to hang over his black service belt. The third man, dressed in a half-buttoned Hawaiin shirt and old jeans jammed into the tops of black Wellingtons has the keen look of someone who has spent his seventy-or-so years wrestling a living from the island or the sea around it.

Fisherman, Ace thinks. *Part time handyman, crab and oyster man.*

"We'd like to be of help," Ace says. "Where can we go to do that?"

The older officer nods his head down the road beyond more wrecked houses and stripped trees to where a large yellow helicopter is descending.

"Old stone church down there next to the lot where the choppers are landing is a makeshift staging point," he says. "High school farther down the road, usually our staging point, didn't do so well. Either of you got any medical training?"

"I'm a retired lawyer," Ace says. He nods at J'nelle. "But she taught sanitation and first aid in the Peace Corps and now does volunteer work with refugees."

"Lawyer?" the man in the Hawaiian shirt says. "Well, you're pretty much useless, but she might be some count to people."

"Go on down there," the heavyset officer says. "They can put you to work."

The young officer tosses the football from one hand to the other and gives them a quick smile as he nods agreement.

Ace and J'nelle say thanks and start down the road. Ace turns.

"You all don't by any chance know what happened last night with the Red Sox do you?"

"Lost one-zip," the younger officer says, still tossing the football. "Headed to LA for game three."

"Shit," Ace says under his breath.

"That new ace pitcher they got—what's-his-name, Aguilla—pulled something in his shoulder. Season's over for him."

"Thanks." Ace turns back toward J'nelle. "Double shit."

"You're a Red Sox fan?" she says. "When did that happen?"

"A while back, mostly because I hate the Yankees."

"That explains a lot."

"What does that mean?"

"Boston fans think they are always getting screwed by gremlins or some other supernatural force. They're committed pessimists."

"So let me guess: you're a Yankees fan?"

"Yes, but mostly I just root against Boston."

The church is not a large building, but its cobblestone exterior seems fixed to the land upon which it sits. There is a small steeple at one corner with a white-frame cupola and a bell. The church's roof is missing shingles, but otherwise the building seems intact.

They pick their way over and around power poles and debris and pass by search crews in military dress working on either side of the road. Four members of one team gather around a collapsed roof while a large man with sergeant's stripes speaks through a megaphone to whomever might be inside. A military bulldozer clears debris from the road in front of the church and pushes the debris into a ditch on the other side. Over the clink of the dozer's tracks and roar of its engine, comes the metallic scream of the helicopter from the lot beyond the church. As Ace and J'nelle draw closer, the scream dies to the slow whump, whump, whump of the chopper's massive blades.

A scene comes to Ace: A clearing in Vietnam. The downdraft from a Chinook helicopter lays flat the elephant grass around the chopper as it sets down with that rocking motion as if feeling about to be sure of its footing. He is running with other men, his head ducked, one hand holding his helmet on, the other clutching an M-16 he carries for a wounded marine. His eyes are focused on that shiny, boot-worn threshold of the chopper's open door. If he can just get there, get a foothold, and heave himself inside to that shadowy illusion of safety.

Whump, whump go the helicopter blades in the lot next to the church. He looks around. He has come to a halt in the middle of the road.

J'nelle walks a few steps ahead, then turns and looks back at him with that look of curious concern he first saw on their beach walk when she told him about her affair and Mason Morrel.

"Just need to catch my breath a second," he says.

"We can find a place to sit."

"I'm OK."

Ace looks past her shoulder toward the church. A large black sign hangs between two brick posts in front of the church near the road. Some of its letters are missing.

Oc_an Dr_ve A.M._. _ion C_urch, it says. *Rev__end Ike Hask_l.* Beneath it, dangling from a hook at one end, is a hand-painted sign in smaller print.

Lifeboat Holiness Church

J'nelle turns back to Ace. "That's the church Faye-Marie told us about, where her Uncle Ike is the pastor."

"Yeah," Ace says, "the same guy who talks to the Lord and predicted the storm would miss us."

"At least his church is still there," says J'nelle, "and look at all the people using it."

There is a dazed atmosphere about the area surrounding the church that appears on the faces of the storm's refugees. Some of them mill about, while others sit on the wet ground on ponchos, rain jackets and shower curtains. Nursing mothers hold nipples to babies. Parents clasp the hands of small children. A group of Latino men has gathered among the limbs of a fallen tree. A young black woman, who appears to be in charge of the scene, goes in and out of the church accompanied by two young men, one an officer in military-issue camouflage.

The tattooed woman Ace gave his water to in the supermarket sits on the steps of the church. A group of children, including her own two kids, surrounds her. A cigarette dangles from her fingers. She grabs playfully at the grinning kids with her free hand, then laughs and turns her head away to blow a mouthful of smoke. Her expression is the inverse of the expression on J'nelle's face Saturday when she talked about Anna: one relaxed and happy, the other infinitely sad. Yet the difference between them seems fragile and razor thin.

As they draw closer to the church, they can see Faye-Marie tending to an old man in a wheelchair in the road by a ditch in front of the church. A young girl stands nearby, holding a towel. She watches Faye-Marie with studied attention, then drapes the towel about her neck and bends to help Faye-Marie with the man's legs.

"Hello, Faye-Marie," Ace says. "We are Ace and J'nelle. We were customers of yours at The Whale Head on Saturday."

Faye-Marie glances up at them for a moment and says, "How are y'all," then goes back to work.

The odor of human feces hits Ace when they are still twenty feet from the chair. It carries a suggestion of mud and the rot of death. As they draw closer, he can see the man's soiled trousers and shoes in a heap on the pavement next to the chair. The girl lifts the man's legs off the seat of the chair, one at a time, so Faye-Marie can scrub under them. Two metal basins of water and a plastic bottle of soap are on the pavement at Faye-Marie's feet. Her sleeves are pulled up above her elbows.

She moves her arms gently under the man's legs as she scrubs, then pulls her arms out and drops the

191

shit-stained towel into one of the basins of brown, soapy water. The girl hands her the clean towel.

Faye-Marie takes it, straightens herself, and glances at Ace and J'nelle.

"Yes," she says, "I remember you. Y'all stay safe last night?"

"We did, but our house is gone," says Ace. He glances around him. "Just like these."

The man's skin is dusty brown with a deep red tint, a color Ace has never seen before, and it hangs about his old man's frame. His head is slightly bowed on his neck and pulls taut the tendons that run from his shoulders to the base of his skull. The tendons remind Ace of roots from a large tree with deep hollows between them.

"That's a shame," Faye-Marie says. Her gaze catches up with Ace's as Ace surveys the scene around them. "It's all a shame."

"At least," J'nelle says, nodding toward the church, "help is here, and these people survived."

"Have y'all heard about the new inlet?" Faye-Marie says. "Washed right through the island north of the bridge. Part of the bridge is gone too."

"Good Lord," Ace says.

"Worst storm I've ever seen," Faye-Marie says, "by far. Looks like we're all going to be here awhile."

Ace shoots a glance at J'nelle, then nods toward the church.

"Can we be some help over there?"

"You can help right here," Faye-Marie says. "This is Rosa Mendez." She nods toward the dark-haired girl with the towels, then toward the man in the wheelchair. "And this is Byron Beethoven Burnett. He's been on Pomeiooc Island for over ninety years. He was born in that house over there." Faye-Marie nods down the road in the direction from which Ace and J'nelle have just come. "They got him out early this morning."

The small house is mostly gone except for a shed-roofed room on the side.

"I need to get him up from this chair and wash off his butt and the chair seat. You reckon you can help Rosa raise him up and hold him?"

"Sure," J'nelle says, stepping forward. "We can do that."

She goes to one side of the chair. Ace follows and stands at the other. The feces smell smears the air, soaks into clothing, clings to the skin. Ace thinks of the smell of dead bodies zipped into body bags and stacked like cordwood in a jungle clearing in Vietnam, waiting for a chopper. Some had been there for four days cooking in the tropical sun. There could be bodies here, in some of the collapsed houses. Zip them into body bags too.

"Take him under his armpits?" Ace says.

"That's right," Faye-Marie says. "Rosa will stand in front and take his wrists and pull from there. Y'all raise him up on either side."

She bends close to Byron Beethoven's ear and says in a loud voice: "Mr. Burnett, these people are here to help you. They're going to raise you up so I can get you clean. Don't you try to fight 'em now. They're good people."

Ace and J'nelle give each other a quick glance before they bend to grasp Byron Beethoven Burnett under his arms. Mixed with the smell of feces is the sour stench of urine. And then there is that old man smell, dry and cold, that exhales from the maw of age.

Rosa grasps the man's wrists and holds his arms out straight.

"Y'all ready?" Faye-Marie says.

"Yes," Ace and J'nelle say together.

"I'm ready," Rosa says.

Freeing Byron Beethoven from his chair releases even more of the odor. His legs are slack and useless. As thin as he is, he is tall, and his weight, concentrated in great lengths of bone, comes as a surprise.

When Ace, J'nelle, and Rosa have Byron Beethoven vertical, Faye-Marie kneels by the chair and goes to work, wiping Byron's buttocks and lifeless genitals, then the backs of his long, boney thighs. She hums as she works, a spiritual Ace recognizes but cannot name, then begins to tell them about Byron Beethoven's sideline as a blues guitar player.

"Played all up and down the coast," she says. "That's how he got his stage name, Beethoven. Had a good voice too. Did a lot of hammer-down—had a real knack with it. Guitar players came from all over to watch how he did it. Played until he was almost ninety, when his mind started to go. He'd prop himself on his stool and play and sing all night."

Ace looks down at Byron Beethoven's wide hands

and slim fingers, long enough to cover five frets on a guitar neck with ease.

Faye-Marie gives Byron Beethoven's knee a soft squeeze. "You were good, weren't you, Mr. Burnett? You're going to be alright. We'll fix you up as good as new."

She throws out the dirty water from the basin, refills it with rainwater left in the ditch by the storm, and squirts in a stream of soap. Byron's head continues to hang forward so that for a moment Ace wonders if he has passed out or maybe even died.

Near the church, a large generator starts and fills the air around them with a deep-throated hum. An ache spreads from Ace's left shoulder, down his arm to the hand gripping the man's limp body under the armpit. His knuckles press hard into the man's ribs, but Byron does not seem to notice. *This is what it's like if you make it this far,* Ace thinks. *Hands holding you that you can't even feel.*

Rosa's grip is strong and steady. Her eyes focus on Faye-Marie's hands as they work to scrub Byron. Faye-Marie finishes with Byron, dashes a basin of clean water over the chair seat, and wipes it dry.

"Thanks y'all," she says. "Set him down easy."

They let Byron Beethoven down into his chair. As he settles in, he raises his head, looks about at the four of them with his rheumy eyes, then looks down at his naked crotch and boney legs. His hand, hanging over the arm of his chair, starts to shake. Faye-Marie takes it in hers and gives it a squeeze.

"I'm Faye-Marie Haskell, Mr. Burnett. I've been knowing you a long time." She reaches out and takes Rosa's hand. "And this is my friend, Rosa Mendez. And these folks are nice people from the island who stopped by to help you."

She straightens and lets go of his hand. "We need to get him over to the church," she says to Rosa. "Take him into the bathroom where we can clean him up some more. Then we'll find him some clean clothes and something to eat."

"Take this to cover him," J'nelle says. She shucks off her rain jacket and gives it to Faye-Marie.

Rosa releases the brake on Byron Beethoven's wheelchair and begins to push him down the road around the uncleared limbs toward the driveway to the church parking lot. The breeze off the sound blows away the lingering stench.

"Mr. Burnett's main line of work was a carpenter," says Faye-Marie. "He built a lot of these homes." She nods toward the wrecked houses down the road from the church. "Helped build the church too."

She empties the basins into the weeds beside the road, swirls the soiled towels around in the watery ditch, and begins to wring them out.

"People on this island think a lot of Mr. Byron Beethoven Burnett." She casts a glance at J'nelle and Ace. "People of all races."

She finishes wringing out the towels and drops them into one of the basins.

"I appreciate the help," she says. "It would have

been hard for Rosa and me to do it on our own."

"It's kind of you to do that for him," J'nelle says. "I suspect there aren't many people around who would take that on."

"I do it all the time," Faye-Marie says. "I'm the one who sees after folks like Mr. Burnett around here."

She reaches for Byron Beethoven's soiled trousers and long-john underwear, rinses them as well, then drops them into the other basin. Ace notes the round curve of her back, the soft roll of flesh where her neck meets her shoulders. Her energy seems to concentrate there and feed the strength and quickness in her arms and hands.

She lifts the basin holding the towels and begins to follow Rosa as Rosa turns Byron Beethoven's chair from the road into the church driveway.

"If y'all don't mind, grab that other basin of Mr. Burnett's clothes and come on; if you still want to help, there's plenty to do."

Ace picks up the basin with the soiled clothes, and he and J'nelle hurry to catch up. Ace speaks loudly to be heard over the revving of a nearby bulldozer.

"The people you help are very lucky to have you," he says to Faye-Marie.

Faye-Marie stops in the road and turns toward them. Her eyes are slightly squinted as if to get Ace and J'nelle in better focus. She studies them a moment.

"I do it because I love them," she says, "and because they are children of God. I look forward to cleaning up their messes like we did with Mr. Burnett. It gives me a chance to pass on the love."

She holds them in her gaze. Ace's mind races back to the scene in The Whale Head: he and J'nelle, seated at the table by the window, wrapped in their conversation about God and their beliefs or lack of belief. He can see himself sitting there, silhouetted against the window, holding his wine glass, spouting his half-baked bullshit about religion and his rejection of all things holy. How loud was he talking? Did Faye-Marie overhear him?

On the road behind him, a bulldozer, pushing a large pile of debris, guns its engine. Its steel treads squeak and clank. Ace glances over his shoulder, then back at Faye-Marie.

Her face relaxes into a smile. "Sometimes," she says, "I get a little carried away."

"No," says J'nelle. "It's wonderful—what you just said, what you do. It's really wonderful."

Faye-Marie turns back toward the church.

"Y'all come on," she says. "There's a place we can wash our hands, see who else needs help—whatever we got to give."

Ace and J'nelle work through the morning at the church. Ace talks with adults and families, explains evacuation plans to them, tells them where the helicopters will take them if they are evacuated inland, directs them to the National Guard medical station in the yard for treatment if they are injured. J'nelle works with the medics and a volunteer civilian doctor and treats minor injuries. Faye-Marie is everywhere. She seems to see the invisible hurt in people and knows how to help them before they understand the hurt themselves.

Pastor Ike Haskell wanders about, talking to the people. Occasionally he places a hand on someone's shoulder or head and prays in a deeply resonant voice that seems to carry beyond the gathering of refugees and out over the sound and the noise of the circling helicopters.

Monday afternoon

Near one p.m., Ace and J'nelle find a spot where the grassy backyard of the church slopes to meet the sound. They sit on a washed-up packing crate to eat peanut butter sandwiches provided to volunteers by women in the church. The aqua-blue water stretches before them, tipped in silver by the midday sun. An arm of the sound wraps around the point where they sit and cuts into the island through a marsh of mauve-tinted needle grass and gray yaupon. Lazy waves, loaded with bits of splintered wood and plastic, a small beach ball, and the ragged remnants of a crab net with the buoy still attached, slosh against the bank at their feet. Amidst the debris, the carcass of a white pelican, a wreck of bony wings and beak, gently rises and falls.

"It's odd," J'nelle says, "all this devastation, yet the air seems so clean, the water so quiet and peaceful."

"Storms do that," Ace says, "they leave a little token for destroying the neighborhood."

Above them, gulls, now out of hiding from the storm, hover as if suspended in the air. J'nelle speaks through a bite of sandwich.

"After we went to our separate bunks last night, I thought about your old case that haunts you and my memory of the time I slapped Anna, and it struck me how vividly we remember the horrifying details, like the imprint of my slap on Anna's face and the condition of that young woman's body. Those details seemed to burn like hot coals in the tight little space of that bunker, long after the words we used to describe them had died. That memory of slapping Anna haunted me all night."

"Memory remembers pain," Ace says. "Back in Old England, before there were surveyors and real estate lawyers, there was a practice called 'beating the bounds,' as a way to teach the eldest son of a landowner, the presumptive heir, the boundaries of the estate. They'd walk him around the boundary, show him the posts and corners, then make him run it naked while they beat him with willow sticks. The pain ensured he'd remember."

"What a nice custom," she says. "At least you lawyers have made some progress since then."

"I'm not so sure," he says. "Apparently they had fewer boundary disputes back then than we do."

"And it's odd," she says, "the other memories, the pleasant ones and the not-so-bad ones, seem less certain. I'm not sure I trust them as much."

"Why, because they weren't branded by pain?"

"I think it's more that I don't trust myself to remember them accurately. Like you said Friday night on your deck, when we started this memory journey: I catch myself lying."

In the distance across the sound, a helicopter drones as if pulling behind it a long string of time. Her voice seems to trail after it.

"That Christmas Eve memory we talked about at lunch the other day, of the cops and the graveyard, do you think it really happened that way?"

Ace takes a bite of sandwich. "I remember the cops and the graveyard and making out on the grave and that for whatever reason, we did not consummate our one and only attempt at carnal union. And that, for Layton, Alabama, even in a midwinter graveyard, it was very cold."

The helicopter comes in close and passes above them, headed down the island. Its downdraft sends a tremble across the water.

"I had not thought about that evening in years," she says. "Then I attended a daylong workshop called 'Rediscovering Your Past, Searching for the Things You've Left Behind.' It stirred up a lot of stuff. I went home exhausted and fell into a troubled sleep. Way into the night, I dreamed about us and the cops and the graveyard. Everything was there in vivid detail, the shadowy interior of the car and smell of wool on our bodies while we were making out before Reggie showed up with his trusty flashlight, the icy pebbles under my feet as I led you through the moonlight to Zebulon Fitts's grave. It was like living through that night again. It was so clear and certain, it had to have happened."

"It was vivid when you related it," he says, "right down to the feel of your body under that dress."

"You remember that little detail?" she says.

"I couldn't swear it happened that night, but it must have happened somewhere."

"Are you sure it happened 'somewhere,' even?"

He gives her a sideways glance. "What do you mean?"

"I mean that maybe, because you like the idea so much, you made it up."

Ace thinks back to breezy nights on the upper deck of his beach house when he sat with a glass of Scotch and let his thoughts drift back to the young J'nelle. The images of her rose to him from the distant past, like those slow-moving headlights coming toward him across the Crowbank Inlet Bridge: her shadowed breast, the flash of her smile, the feel under his sliding hand of that long muscle inside her thigh. And smells, too: body heat, powdered flesh, smeared Clearasil. And sounds: heavy breathing, quick gasps, the slide of clothes on skin. Those thoughts created a sensory force that wanted more images, smells, and sounds. So he searched. And were they there in his memory waiting to be found, or did he pull them from the vast, oceanic darkness?

"I don't know," he says. "But it's a very pleasant idea, and I'm sticking with it."

"Exactly," she says. "I have a psychologist friend who interprets dreams. She says that Christmas Eve dream that seemed so real was a twilight of life dream where you search back over your life for things you've lost or let pass you by. They're often dreams of deep longing, and I suspect that in that dream, I changed that memory to how I needed it to be."

"So you don't trust it," he says.

"I don't trust all the details, but I trust the dream because it led me to what I was searching for."

"Which is?"

"The magic in that moment. I wanted to recapture that magic when we were young and innocent and I knelt on that cold ground and looked up at your silhouette above me in the moonlight and pulled you down to me. That moment was so precious and deeply intimate, so full of joy and hope, longing and fear. It was all there in that instant, and we were there in it. And then it was gone."

Her voice trails off. Ace strains to recall those feelings she has just described, her hands held out to him as she knelt on the grave, the warm feel of them in the cold night, the tightening of her fingers on his as she pulled him down to her. Those feelings, light as a feather yet laden with a million things he did not understand, called to him from the kneeling girl, reaching out to him, beckoning him to adventure and another life.

"I had no idea what was right there before me," he says. "I had no idea what we had."

"No," she says. "It was both of us, and what a waste— something that fragile and precious entrusted to the ineptitude of youth."

"So what should we have done to save it?" He turns back to face the sound, takes a bite of sandwich and speaks through a mouth full of peanut butter. "Or maybe the question is, should we have done anything to save it?"

204

The drone of the helicopter fades. A lone gull hovers nearby. Its calls seem tentative, far away.

"Sometimes," she says, "I wish we'd made love all over that grave."

He turns to look at her. She is still facing the water. Sunlight reflects from it onto her chin and lips and the bridge of her nose.

"And gotten pregnant?" he says.

"It would have been risky; it could have happened."

"You've really thought about this?" he says.

"Yes."

"So I got you pregnant—and then what?"

"Then our parents would have thrown a fit, and our names would have been mud, and we would have had to drop out of school and get jobs and learn to care for a baby and struggle to make it, and it probably would have all turned to shit. But looking back, it was a chance I'd be willing to take. Who knows, it might have worked."

The gull is above them now, its cry softer and more mewling, waiting Ace suspects for a scrap of sandwich.

"Probably not," he says, "given your attitude toward cooking and housework."

"I'm good at washing dishes."

The gull moves on. The breeze dies. The sound lies quiet under the bright sun. Ace shifts his weight on the packing crate.

"But we didn't make love all over that grave," he says. "For whatever reason, we chickened out. We left those kids and their magical moment behind. It's gone, they're gone, and we can't go back and get them. So what's the point of going over it all again? It doesn't really get us anywhere."

"Maybe," she says, "our revisiting that story is where the dance we now find ourselves in really began."

She looks down at her half-eaten sandwich and then at him. "Right?"

Ace finishes his last bite and crushes the wax paper into a ball. It feels like a wad of every second and every moment since she arrived. He stuffs it in his pocket and turns to gaze into the long corridors of her eyes, lit in their soft hews of green and blue. But the corridors lead to no exit and have no end.

"J'nelle," he says, "I need you to tell me the real reason you came down here—please."

She turns back toward the sound and assumes that same faraway look she had that night almost sixty years ago at the carhop drive-in when she told him to take her home—now! That mystery in the shape of her, sitting next to him in the car.

"I had to do something," she says, "to get out of my life."

Like she tried to do with Mason Morrel, joining the Peace Corps, marrying Seth—maybe even the night she led him from the car to the grave and pulled him down to her.

Once again, he thinks of himself on his roof deck watching the endless stream of headlights. That image from T.S. Eliot's *The Waste Land* comes floating back to him, of soulless people crossing London Bridge: "I had not thought death had undone so many."

Footsteps squish on the rain-soaked lawn behind them. He glances over his shoulder to see Faye-Marie. She comes to a halt with her fists on her hips and looks out over the sound. Her jeans are rolled above her ankles; her red tennis shoes are flecked with black mud.

"I love this spot," she says. "I come here a lot in the evenings since Travis, my husband, died. I stand and look out over the water. That is, when the mosquitos aren't so bad."

"Sorry to hear about Travis," J'nelle says. "When did he pass?"

"He was killed in Iraq," Faye-Marie says, "twelve years ago. Flew helicopters—just like the ones we're seeing today. That's where I met him, in the military."

"You were in the military?" Ace says.

"Yes," Faye-Marie says. "Twenty years."

"What did you do?"

"I was part of an analyst team. We plotted targets."

"For artillery, missiles?"

"Drones."

"Oh yeah," Ace says. "I imagine that's tricky business."

"Yes," Faye-Marie says, "it is—real tricky."

Ace is about to say he was once a target-plotter in the artillery in Vietnam, when Faye-Marie continues in a voice one might use to explain the death of a parent to a child.

"One day we got a target wrong, very wrong, and a bunch of innocent people died."

The waves, kicked up by a helicopter downblast, slosh louder against the bank. The dead pelican bobs

207

amidst the debris, its shank of a beak pressed into its chest, eyes shut like an old man in sleep.

"Poor people mostly," Faye-Marie says, "with children. I couldn't do it anymore. They were about to discharge me, but my commanding officer talked them into letting me train as a medic to get in my twenty years. I liked that; it was better to care for people than to kill them."

"Sometimes," Ace says, "the army gets it right."

"Air force," Faye-Marie says.

"Wherever you learned it," J'nelle says, "you're very good at it now."

"Thank you," Faye-Marie says. "I try." She pauses, then drops back into her prayerful tone. "In the evenings when I'm here alone, the souls of those people call to me, and I weep for them. And then Travis comes to comfort me. I feel his arms around me, and then I feel the presence of the Lord."

Ace feels the day recede around him, leaving him at the dead center of it.

"That's wonderful," J'nelle says. She spreads her free hand open on her thigh, then balls it slowly into a fist. Ace touches the back of it with the tips of his fingers.

"I'm sorry," Faye-Marie says. "I didn't mean to get into all that. I guess something about that storm got to me."

"Yes," Ace says. "It got to me too."

They fall into a moment's silence until Faye-Marie speaks.

"Are y'all married?"

"No," Ace says. "We're just good friends."

"Uh, huh," Faye-Marie says. "Just friends."

"Old friends from high school," J'nelle says. "We just got together this weekend to rehash old memories."

"Did you get them figured out?" Faye-Marie says.

"Not sure," Ace says.

"You want an outside opinion?"

"Well," Ace says, "I guess it wouldn't hurt."

Faye-Marie clears her throat. Her voice settles like a net over them.

"You're a lot more than just friends from high school."

Ace closes his hand over J'nelle's fist and gives it a squeeze. Finally, Faye-Marie says: "Well, I've got to get back. Y'all come on when you can. I brought some key lime pie from the restaurant. I saved you a piece."

Ace waits for Faye-Marie to get out of hearing and nudges J'nelle.

"I may not believe in God," he says, "but I believe in Faye-Marie."

"Amen." J'nelle wraps the remains of her uneaten sandwich. "I think we just got an invitation to get back to work."

Ace pushes himself off the packing crate and offers J'nelle a hand up, expecting the bony grip they usually share. But her fingers feel soft, with a delicate tension that reminds him of the night she took his hands at the grave.

She lets go, brushes the crumbs from her lap, and gazes intently across the sound.

"What kind of building was that?" She points to the skeleton of a wrecked building on a distant point. What's left of the building's white siding glows in the sun.

"An old hotel," Ace says.

"I think," she says, "that's the hotel where Seth and Anna and I stayed when we came down here in '79. It was on a point like that, jutting into the sound, and had three stories."

"That was it, then," he says, "The Soundside Inn. It was the only three-story building on the island. About the same vintage as my house."

The thumping roar of another helicopter passes over them as it makes its way to somewhere farther down the island. J'nelle continues to stare at the wrecked hotel, her lips pressed thin and tight. Ace takes her hand. She barely seems to notice.

"You're going to keep looking for her, aren't you?" he says.

"Yes," she says. "That's just the way it goes."

"Would you like some help?"

She gives him a startled stare.

"Why would you put yourself through that?"

"Why did you stay with me last night?"

"I haven't quite figured that out yet."

"To get out of your life, you said a minute ago."

"That's why I came, not why I stayed."

Now it's he who stares out at the sound. "I was awake last night too," he says. "I've never shared the shame of that case with anyone before except Pam. But it felt good, like I had thrown open that metal bunker door and let some air and light in. I thought about how that feeling compared to the way I felt the night before when I was being swallowed in that rip current, and I realized that it's not death I fear most, it's being alone."

Her eyes focus intently on his face.

"That's not quite right," he says. "What I'm really afraid of is being alone without you."

She bows her head in that now familiar way, revealing a part in her hair he has not noticed before, where the hair is thin and colorless, almost opaque, very different from the luxuriant wings that fall to her shoulders. He thinks of his own thinning hair, mere wisps of what it used to be. It's as if the strands themselves shrink.

She raises her face to him. Her blue-green eyes shimmer behind a thin veil of tears.

Just like the times she cried in high school, he has no idea what to say.

She runs a finger under her nose and glances toward the church. "Maybe we should get back to work."

"Wait a minute," he says and takes her arm. "Can't you at least say something in response to what I just said?"

She takes a deep, moist breath. "OK, then what?"

"Then what, what?"

"After you join me to search for Anna, then what?"

They walk side by side. He's on the edge of the cotillion dance floor again, across the reunion lawn.

"I guess then," he says, "it will be, 'Your place or mine?'"

She gives him another stare.

"You mean one of us leaves where we are and just moves in?"

"Why not?"

"Well, I can think of a few reasons: we've both got results from major medical tests hanging over our heads, just out of cell phone reach. They could mean all sorts of things that could be, well, bad. And what, if by some miracle, I find Anna and have to spend the rest of my life caring for her, watching her every move?"

"If I've learned anything this weekend," he says, "it's that I'm ready to quit worrying over 'what-ifs.'"

Her lips, tight again, tighter than any time he can remember this weekend. "It's rash and risky," she says.

"For sure," he says, "like the walks on the beach, the candlelight and music, the midnight swim, this whole fucking weekend."

An osprey hovers above the sound, not far offshore. Ace wonders if it is the same late-migrater they saw on Friday from his upper deck, as it dove to catch a fish— just after she arrived at the house, before she delivered the news to him about her and Mason Morrel, before anything that has passed between them in the last four days happened. Those first moments together back there on the upper deck when the deck was intact and timeless and part of a progression that, in spite of his warnings about the house being doomed, he imagined would go on forever. They were there, he and J'nelle, when the osprey dove and took the fish. His hands rested on the weatherworn pine railing. She stood next to him, her glowing hair lifted off her shoulders by the wind. The pulse of that long-ago Christmas Eve night beat its way toward them through the years.

In the distance, far beyond the osprey, a lopsided V of cormorants moves dart-like across the sky.

"The large birds are back," he says.

She crosses her arms, stares at her feet.

"If you don't want to do this," he says, "just say so."

She resumes her walk across the yard toward the church. Once again, he hurries to catch up. "You said yourself that it was your story at The Whale Head that got this dance started. What did you expect would happen?"

He reaches for her arm and turns her to face him. From the corner of his eye, he can see Faye-Marie and a couple of other women watching them from the edge of the crowd at the church.

"I mean, seriously," he says. "If you didn't want us to wind up here, what was the point?"

J'nelle blinks her eyes clear.

"OK," she says. "Yes."

"Yes to what?"

"To 'Your place or mine?'"

"Jesus," he says. "I have a hard time keeping up with you."

"For a while at first, OK? Just to see how it goes."

"Of course."

Her lips break in the slightest hint of a smile, the shyest thing he's ever seen from her.

"I think we'll be OK," she says, "but there are lots of

things to work out. We're at the end of long, complicated, other-lives, and they don't just go away."

"The cling of the past," he says.

"Yes. And then there's the present day stuff: what to do about your beach house, test results, financial arrangements, and ultimately, 'your place or mine?'"

"Not to mention the small details," he says, "like your disdain for cooking and resistance to terms of endearment."

"And the fact," she says, "that you're still in love with another woman."

The size of the crowd at the church has overflowed into the road, where more refugees make their way past bulldozers and work crews to join it. A helicopter, loaded with people bound for the mainland, lifts off and passes over Ace's and J'nelle's heads. It moves out over the sound, blades thumping the air.

"I guess," says Ace, "we've worked ourselves into something of a mess, haven't we?"

"It won't be perfect."

"No," he says, "it won't. But it looks like we'll be here for a while, so we've got plenty of time to work our way out of it."

Her soft, nimble fingers interlace with his, finding their way among the cartilaginous bumps and knuckles.

"Sugar," she says, "we already have."

ACKNOWLEDGMENTS

Lots of people helped me write this book. Foremost is my wife, Betsy, a fountain of positive energy and lifter of spirits who was ever-willing to read and critique another draft. Friend Craig Nova read the entire manuscript, and his comments were, as always, invaluable. More than that, he provides fire-in-the-gut inspiration and rock-solid encouragement for the writing life. Lee Smith is the most generous writer toward other writers I know, and I am the lucky beneficiary of her talents as teacher, consummate artist, and model for others. She is another major source of energy behind this book. Judy Goldman was also generous with her help and support. Mary Moore, another good writing friend, read a draft, and her insightful, pointed suggestions resulted in major changes. Others who read all or parts of the many drafts are members of my writing group: Marko Fong, David Lange, Terri Lange, Jack Raper, and Tom Wolf. They are fine writers all, and sharp critics, and their help and encouragement made the difference in those throw-in-the-towel moments.

Nora Gaskin Esthimer of Lystra Books is a splendid editor with that extra gift of patience that helps nudge a writer through the tough edits and changes. She also runs a terrific press. Kelly Lojk is a master at book design and a diamond-sharp copyeditor.

To all of them, I am deeply grateful.